# THE CHRYSALIS TIME

## By Matthew Woods

Matthew Woods

Published by:
Chipmukapublishing
PO Box 6872
Brentwood
Essex
CM13 1ZT
United Kingdom

www.chipmunkapublishing.com

The development of this book was made possible by a grant from The Arts Council, London.

# THE CHRYSALIS TIME

Dedicated to Constance

Matthew Woods

## PART 1 The Caterpillar

## PART 2 The Chrysalis

## PART 3 The Butterfly

Matthew Woods

## PART 1 THE CATERPILLER

### Chapt. 1 This Forfeit Enchantment

Ele'hail was growing, the baby by her mother's side, soon to be plucked from marrow in the land of Miserablenow. The powers of women were engulfing spells for a granddaughter in the village Michael was estranged from. Amaeigin had seen to that. The tyrant's bloodline was thwarted by her very existence. She now stood between his ambition and the throne of Miserablenow. Three looked, alone, into the garden where he and Velouria had sat and talked and romanced for those years as a warbling wren perched elegantly on a fork put there previously. The garden at the top of the Martello tower. Previously the pain was just a dream. Today sorrow was washed away by the rain. Would there be an impact of responsibility to do what we chose and what if that was evil? If we practise choice, it has an effect on others and our relationships. Amaeigin had choices from within which were abominable notions that the wren would recognise then flew to where they know not. Plucked from marrow in the land of Miserablenow; Velouria had placed in others' lives goodness, and in honour and respect Michael followed her. We stared at the writing. I asked her a question. She said yes. I worked like a slave. I planned meticulously like a caterpillar in a pupa- but what to answer?

The Forest Cavern
Peddlers Wood
Frinton
Miserablenow

Dearest Velouria

I love you I do. I have only like for you because I love you so much. I love thee like the silken rose that glories in your gaze. I love thee like the starry night that glistens hope so bright. I love thee like the early dew which cozens and lifts mystery's hue. I love thee like the pastoral harmony's shower which grips your wanton lichen ivory tower. I love thee like honesty pales in moonlight, garters oft to see, I love thee like the honourable kiss we shared that moment of constant glee. I love thee like the bliss we had that I shall often miss. I would disregard the brightest star for you. Climb a mountain knowing never to return if only I had your eyes in my mind. Never is forever. Our victims are strewn about by the obsequious fervour of a spider building a web of protection with a sequinned edge- how do you like it? Writing to the princess I was with today, dark eyes so demure next to delicate white skin, but on fire like the cities of Miserablenow under Viking advance. As I prepare to give in under gravity and rush up to your tower, I only feel the need to ask if gravity keeps you warm in bed? Does it fade like yesterday's news where I'm the story of a lacklustre performer and you are the spark of decorum in modern religion, proud in its exasperating naivety? I know now that we are not yesterday's news and that the girl who lost her face at some stranger's place is just a wave of mutilation I must endure for having the surf in my eye, when it's much more my style to have sand kicked in it.

Now that it's within my reach I will rise as you fall and not deny you this, my bleeding heart. Now that it's within my reach, stuck between the do or die, I will show you the space of a thousand golden sunsets, every colour you are, the warmth of a spring shower, blessed with all the thunder in the world, the whispers of a classroom of schoolboys upon the delights of the music teacher's legs who only wants to be loved. I want you and that kiss was breathtaking, as though you had shined your headlamps upon a frightened rabbit and in one fluid gesture saw through my disguise and decided to swerve and use your breaks. Any harder or faster I would have been forever after just roadkill but you stopped and picked me up ready to nurse me back to health by your kiss. For that my lips are grateful. It fills me with gladness, the dream that comes alive at night, the tantalizing fascination that I've even had once or twice, but being with you is enough. Cut to a scene in a small pastel coloured room that I will never forget.

Our identity has not stopped what is coming. You know when I said I often turn around and notice that there's no one there at all well there often is, Amaeigin's spies, and I therefore find it hard to relate to the kind of life we deserve. Freedom instead of going around hiding our love. However, I've told Methuselah from the start. I told anyone who'd listen that I was obsessed with you. You have been a temptress for too long; a femme fatale who has found ferocity but also a fragility, which most men will exploit. From the shadow you call and I declare that I will find a way. I wish no more than to learn to love you more and more, and tenderly take your lies and wish them away. As for Xtopherus's mission the eroticism is far too dangerous to include you at the moment, he is the double agent and I am only a novice but given the opportunity to turn you, must show a degree of respect for my professional ability. The most important lesson is not to convert from queen and country and these kisses will foam the bath of spying, bubbles as driven snow. I know that this will happen as I believe in the certainty of chance. There is much I will never be able to anticipate in you; you are far too mysterious and deep for that but I am not scared anymore. For a spy must show no fear yet be insecure enough to see the truth:

Sometimes at night the darkness and silence plays on me. Peace frightens me. Perhaps I fear it most. I feel it is only a façade, hiding the face of hell. I think about what is in store. The world will be wonderful, they say- but from whose viewpoint? We need to live in a state of suspended animation like a work of art; in a state of enchantment, detached. I long to make love with Angel' rain and find out how she felt on the fields of green. This truth is that which dawned on me as I was driven home last night, that we are spies, for queen and country, but moreover a spy who has fallen in love with you. We are both members of a secret society. Please don't think that I am a charlatan for though I am trying to convert you and have been monitoring your conversations with other men, known as spies for the new world order, the poignancy of your words has not fallen on deaf ears. Down your hallowed paths I am young again and our love is so strong it moves objects in my house. One day you will be your own, and as for me all I want is to be your possession. I long to tear the swastika from your eyes and hopefully we will see a bit of Miserablenow when we find what love we bore for, what remains and what has changed shimmering under the sun.

*Nor Miserablenow did I know till then, what love I bore for thee, among thy mountains did I feel, the joy of my desire, and she did cherish, beside a Miserable fire, by morning showed, the night concealed the bough where Angel' rain played and my heart the last green field that her eyes survey around the earth's diurnal course With rocks and stones and trees she treads among the untrodden paths.* ©Blake

I am afraid that you have been duped rather by Amaeigin who is a hollow, callous creature who has dazzled the populace with confusion and kindness, pretty words in the face of Viking advance. You can choose to believe others or trust in me, the good in Ele'hail will show you the moment of truth in your lies and the bad will bleed you just to know you're alive. I will never say that all you can breathe is my life, nor ever be fully aware of your preciousness. But as Tori says *You bet your life it is, you swear to Christ you won't, on your life you won't, but it seemed like a good solution hanging with the raisin girl.* I'm not saying I don't need to disentangle my life more but my loyalty is yours and it goes without saying that this letter is supposed to keep you from those with the evil intent, as I am intent upon protecting your honour but not the rights of girls/blokes who want to take their clothes off. You need my voice to soothe you though I know you dwell on higher things- I hope to the dandelion wish that you do not mistake that which controls you for me. For the fear will dissipate like smoke one day.

The orgasmatron is out to get me, waiting on the line. You said you were serious so this is a serious letter. I've found the one I was waiting for and I will never let go until the seas run dry and the earth stops turning. I am no longer content to remain friends, though I'll bow to your better judgment, in time, if it has to be. You said I make you smile and I reside in your smile. Luck has followed me about all day and I'm convinced of the strength you instil in me. Your faith touches me like a fire in my being and although the photographs of the past will slowly fade away like all tomorrow's yesterday's my latent fears will become desire, if only you say you'll go out with me. There I've asked you. You would honour me more than the wisdom of speech and the haunting of past pride ever could if you would be gracious enough to accept. I was left wanting last night and I expected you just to give which was selfish. Sorry. This could be really something though.

I have something to confess and my catholic guilt complex probably sees you a virgin princess so I better not trust in the Lord for guidance or I'll end up like poor Erol in a ditch starring at the stars. I couldn't get the images you evoked out of my head on the journey home and the one conjured under the tree, erected my world -making love to you, by the spiral trees (maybe you thought a chemical high would let me catch up on some sleep) but I'm telling you that for one and a half hours later I felt I was levitating; haven't felt that good in ages, ever. I felt reunited with myself and as though my soul went on a journey, feeling as though I could feel my soul move inside me. It kind of arose and conversed the ancient ways. I've never really felt like this over a girl before and it's all down to the emotions you bring out in me. If only you'd give us the chance I'd wrap you up in cotton wool and love you like a real man should, show you the glories of yesterday, the spinning delights of today and the interest of a thousand different futures. One of which is with me surely?

I implore you to pick that one, as you'd make me the proudest, or at least as proud as anyone who has been out with you before. I'm not saying I could reach the heights of misdirected passion but I can sympathise actually. Maybe when you're a famous musician and I'm a famous writer we could outbid the rest and buy passion for safekeeping and you could have my children and live happily ever after. But I start at the foot of the rainbow, the end of coincidence with a shower of gold, which I will spend for romance and for only romance's sake. I dare not spite the astral temptress who pulled our strings by being too full of soul's hope nor desolate of my pretensions with which I can easily use to turn an opportunity into ordinariness. We triumphed in the snow, its delicacy our love and its beauty our love, burning Christianity in your big and balmy bed to find that it was indeed the temple of our souls' harbour, not built by hands, not contained by man. Now that I have bought our fantasies from the market place with the croc of gold I feel content at the end of the working day. I would get ridiculed for being too tall if I spoke of the things we have to gain and though I have told you often of being a fool I can roll with the punches. Such is love's foolish notions. If flight or fight emotions rise in you just don't be scared. We have found each other and that is all that matters.

Love and Green

Michael

Bitter leaves love sweet as mandrake so let that river that runs from the forest to the tower smote the iron neath reproduction of mighty yore and cross at break necked speed over to the sea. As he walked towards the shoreline his thoughts to Velouria went, swinging sweet languid wishes, flung upon wing neath innocent flow, a father's moon beam sailing upon a sea resplendent glowing, scattering light into their dark sentiments towards this familiar shore. "My thoughts to you keep- lightening, deepening our souls deny upon feet neath innocence seep a wishes bream upon the tide. I walk on a carpet of shells this whip of dreams embarks pain that spans the ocean deep seems as nothing upon this crystal shore. For lonely I am but never; coming seeping flowing together gathering expressions like the tide I trust the joy of yesterday's gathering that descends like clouds on the horizon sways and fans the wake of my ship- pain that spans the ocean deep seems as nothing upon this new page, just as the circling of birds."

Cover our black bushels with innocence and take care and heed the mountain's rivulets and crest of the wood-mandrake-seas to service those relations that respectfully flow in the riverbed. A message, time after time to fiercely remember each postulated honeydew corn wish to refresh each morn-monumental gesture of chicken-bloodied weir neath eyes of the fireflies' skies struck asunder by the seed of fixed joy, touched by the room of the secret child and stone mandrake guarding her, gargoyle of my thoughts, memories in the shadows as the river flows from me to you. Michael made his way to the forest and came across the women praying and chanting by the shore and forest edge.

The women are whispering. Something tells someone in the gagalamair of grasses the rub of ointment gently into a leaf and throwover shawl. Someone tells somebody in the glory of a buttercup the nuance of an ant into a spider's crazy web. Memories in the shadows. Somebody tells somewhat gainst a rabbit-warrened oak to let the water riff over forgotten wicked wishes. Somewhat tells no-one of tainted love to delude the soul in its developing insecurity. A child and Velouria locked in the highest ivory tower of Walton by her wicked stepfather Amaeigin when he learnt of her pregnancy. Michael remained just the king of the buttercups.

The women spoke: "This child of buttercups as each of us wishes our poetry to be everlasting, float between me and you in vows of trust -an axe that in grass rusts beyond friendship of the fair, ghost to crow we dare to fly a shaft of glorious sound across your page I found character and words become one, drifting in our expressions- musical vowels for longer than the great silver slumber thread of time. The very air she breathes. In its quivering wake time moves faster than wings to caste, drift slower than sails to low. The speed of the spell of chrysalinity. Clamour as amour to butter yellow star of faith finds our four-leaf clover in folds of gaiety big as crushed as the sun's ardour's strength of penitentiary length a stable farm's husbandry snow-blind love, pale away from the hunger like birds' shimmy in alarm by razing his always rising quest to flourish in the meadow by borrowed love. Bless this childbirth and deliver us this forfeit enchantment in this heir."

The tainted king by morning cries with joy and despair and by night lights up the sky, underneath the old oak carousel. A halo of buttercups raised above his head bats beaten like candyfloss in orchard-blue sky he sat with ages and eyes astride the burning font of the inner authority he employed. Like that rubbery toffee apple ripening in the sun with forelocks on fire spreading will opens circle- wolves find the attraction of air; the fairground lighted sorrows a jack rod of a hat at the top of a hare. Love's pressure takes a flapping route as Oberon sits with blazes laden in berry, harpies' chords under his hands a carriage; he thwarts the feeling akin to gravity. Petulant sweet desire was Michael, treacherous power was Amaeigin.

Oh, daisy give me your answer; like the yin yang moon hovers amidst the dumb-struck shout Ele'hail screams "I keep it all in!" wanted with honey and wished with bats, passion sighing with vibrations for oh for my goose-plucked angel to come home again. Blessed quotes spreading manic nouse burning down the house. Honesty takes the riddle, perched beneath the spreading Wurlitzer.

"To walk with you is bliss, to love you is perfection, to lose you is grand like a mystical last proses in a bed of roses." Michael spoke as he sat at Woodbury Hollow. He had sat many times here since his exclusion from Velouria. His thoughts found expression in the dusk: "Creature comfort is Amaeigin's prize, the luxury problems, that passes as wet clay here. As the nightingale sings over the din I pay for unforgotten sin, the nettle ointment rings out autumn constancy. I miss you when the compass from Miserablenow calls your name with the sleight of hand all in the game. Our myths lend an ear- for will it be the same with a kite of sand lifting my mane? I miss you where the angels fear to tread and call my name with a might of amethyst and rain. May the rain and sun decide to bow and become my shepherds crook over this green and pleasant land." Old sensations rushing in, he had seen the rainbow by the river.

Erecting form from dark regions of the soul two people met; two spectres like lamps quivering, living earth goddess spinning a tapestry of life where living seemed a laugh and love was telling him to stay. Perhaps the elegance of rainbows portrayed the rapture. "Excuse my heart which you kindled and left me standing bleating." When they first met, she stood like a statue the white marble composing virtue and consumed by water pounding upon his grave expression for his soul lay on the river bed. She wore that heart like a faithful promise, incidental to their water borne union their heads bowed in passion's gaze as the river dancing the last fantastic place between a man and a woman, between angels. "There was an angel in your eyes that night neath wings of feathers and chest of gold, plumes of hair neath halo of old; a triumph born in glory of love and honour endeavours to try your patience every now'n again. If it would have been an angel's kiss we'd be sitting still by river and willow majestic, a rainbow between cabined ears forever."

He looked out at the descending forest beneath him. Controversial lesions of pulp drip amber trumpets of resin onto the heated plank on a plain and forest patch. Wipe the resin from my eyes. Cover my elegant passion with dandelion breath neath the pretty boughs. Swaths of memories rustle the red and yellowing phantoms that twirl and laugh at me in my dreams; only figments, pigments of my soul; a soul facing up to reality. My Velouria's brevity to find. Sassy you were and delightful and clean, like the steps of a church. Crazy you had been always enjoying solitary scenes like a well of the dead, closest often seen. Hungry you were like the bluebell array in its heyday. Classic you were like the lines of a statue. Magnificent you were like the heraldry of the songs you sang, hazy like the flowers and gone like the ghosts that listen at the lantern. All in our foggy trip.

Flowers are like faces in a manipulative deplorable blue sky, castigate a stare across the garden, jack-in-a-box wary- Timber! The hole of the knot screamed sporadic spirals of the wooden grain adorable, delicate rings painted by a child. Timber! The camaraderie of men in the shade of jays- a woodcutter's ablutions scattering over Woodbury hollow. My mushroom covered moss bench tells me slowly, tells me quick that to fell this problem- the crow's stand, the butterflies gasp- would be to invest; to peruse the whole vista, lying with my fatherly lever, dancing with her musician's ghost; in her body of wishes, regalia, pleasure respondent to her whims, her charms like Icarus dripping off laden trees.

# THE CHRYSALIS TIME

Once Velouria in a lifetime
Flew above the chimney stacks
Her wings unfurled aglow
Singing sweetly, I miss you
For days without an angel
Are such sweet sorrow

The trees were cross-looming slender forms; the mushroom crushed by flowing gaze risked losing to slip into Pascal's dew to sink to its knees in pity for Velouria to quicken Michael's hand to grant me this. For long have I held study- to rub the feverish toil under the dying sun of autumn. Sought the magpie's wing, the elephant's tusk, this squirrel's silly prance too harsh for this art. For a new life. Ele'hail peaceful and new rather like the deer that chastened my view. Amidst the languor of play and decay, swaying majestically twixt stream and bank. The rocking cradle I await holy and bright, safe and clean, knowing mortalities flight. I long to cradle both in my arms. Michael decided to make his progress from the forest hills to the town. He entered the rows of alms-houses and formal gardens to the din of the market square he followed and he sat composing for his baby who was due to be born in the tower which rose over the marketplace.

This the webbing hour, cockled from its fleece of bluebells, orient amber and jute. Cooled by the black-breasted churl. Opinions linked by a tower of green-gabled palaces, phone spearmint in the sun in a lettuce-stream-cobbled market on fireworks night, between the covers we sit and lie in shadows of my love upon our fears. My workshop honesty will not raise the bread-spirals like cherry dragons of sweat upon your brow our tender trying. You feel her coming. A new vibration, a sensation. From afar you'll see me- so close yet so clear. All that I would be you are. All that I am you will always be. I love you for all eternity, yet as my tea cools, I smile a smile for you- simply my source of joy. The fireworks in the town were heralded by a fire in the marketplace. It cracked into life and this a sound that was to cover the butterfly on the wheel: such bright sparks with softer strings strum on inevitable heartstrings inert, static, immaculate; jumping jack Shoreditch flash spunking money up the wall. Pillars telling of frosted presence of well chilled lizard-lounge cellars stealing trumpets off sparks and lending a magpie ear to a vision: On November 5th-constancy is specially emerged 'neath wings of insect and halo of angel to bounce as beauty basks, creamy dewy lights hand in hand across our vista to the balmy working-week welcome of their reptiles tongue lashes and holds it's cool so gently, so smoothly, so feverishly smiles upon the wasted hill teeters like roses saved from the brink glory of love and honour to fly over this majestic bonfire night. This firework day I explode for the first time since the proms, then I shall see my first serpentine sight of Walton through its glass lens, its rough and ready tower, coffee sandwich stone domes, our film, our scarf, our pawed might, a pipe to calculate me coming down from my pinnacle of light I see the vantage-valley berth; a space between our cabined ears. So, bode the fifth of November well my dears.

Michael could not stand the anticipation. He went out to his forest lair to securely pray for the newborn. There was never pain inside the tunnel of love. My wider lamplight shivers towards the book inside the cave of wood and mould-leafiness inside a well of beauty basking through the canopy. A figure emerges outside this bed of lovers. The nurture binds and creates. Nature's climb of soul outside the pupae of wood and mould. Clambering boys yearn for a dream to be born -see me- feel me- touch me. Dappled dew-blocked bark beneath halo of expression under a swelling sun noon now's obliging ride to dial the moon face, caterpillar to butterfly, to ring up tomorrow and say: "You break my little heart". This the webbing hour, cockled from its fleece. The child Ele'hail was born. My cinnamon girl.

## Chapt. 2 Mother Nature with Nurture Was

As Velouria slumbers we wish for muses and galleons as the sounds from a dragonfly rumble laying scales sung in chorus. We strive to be kind, honourable, brave. Yet. Yet our music is to configure a scenario of justice in darkness. My name is hidden from their night. Velouria was godless and alone. No-one dares penetrate the stone tower. In her clutches Ele'hail. Fires circled her camp of those still loyal to Velouria's family the old guard of Miserablenow that lift that baby right off the ground.

Only to see you gathered on a bed of pearl and roses. See your sky feathered into masked glory billowing from the moon drops of ivory. See the heather in your veil turn to deepest white to flower tenfold on the hills of old. I have a vision of Ele'hail in flight, caught by the wind and soaring in the air pockets. As the sun rose on this, Ele'hail's first day, the countryside flowers beckoned beneath a cushion of bees: The hammer wishes it were a frown and the zephyr in your arms, cushioned in a puzzled garden on its crazy paving. The daisy awaits the bee neath skies of tom-foolery. Shall we start to work our spell? Mother Nature with nurture was a tune in the tears before bedtime. The butterfly flaps lavishly, but the miraculous bee should never neath skies of tom-foolery. Bee

Yet you are, and need not his mignon in the elaborate sanguine familiar world Velouria inhabits. Are not your fears which draw you, nor ego which drives you, your future which awes you, love which soothes you, conscience which guides you, and your heart which rules you? And will not this forgive just as the vessel will not give up its men to the storm but labours on regardless away from the light enhancing future by memories now controlled by the swell? The eyes are away from the lighthouse but not our memories. Dawn is upon us, photographs of a memory. Numbers make a circling bird, fly the words of a transparent thread and I begin to climb to the contours of her face for my baby to satisfy the heart, which dark innocence envelops and constancy sees as uncharted soul, instilled in me like hunger. For a magical secret spent from a lighthouse beam.

Michael wrote a letter to Velouria in his cavern and disguised it in a breakfast parcel he sent via the kitchens.

The Forest Cavern
Peddlers Wood
Frinton
Miserablenow

Nov. ad605

Dear Velouria and Ele'hail

Good fortune and good luck to you both. I have visions of you. Like dimensions which glow and pigment my every hour on this paper trail. Original and unique destiny let us, wonderfully feathered with joy, hope and strength; inspiration's darkness and light as the talent of compassion- have such devotion yet our winding sun-dappled absence has been my rain-black cloud of doubt. Each time I dream of your eyes I find my emotional renewal. I found the meaning, fulfilment, the mind blowing, the comfortable, the tortuous and creepy in the cherished moments I saw you. Give me the strength to be truly, madly, deeply be in love with you Velouria and Ele'hail.

Can you find me space inside your bleeding heart? You know that if you needed help it should come from me and vice-versa. I hoped- was it because we suffered or that we can still realise the moment? That we are prepared; that we have the integrity and reason to keep our love afloat. Yet ghosts of catastrophe and disappointment make such arduous tasks of even the simplest of things. People assume therefore that I am simply weak. See the lonely boy out on the weekend. Can't relate to joy. I find myself in reverie from what we had and might have again through the rigours and energy of the future. All my ghosts are in the past. Lain to rest, my demons conquered. I leave the Halloween lantern as energy given to know I am truly the luckiest man on the planet. So, while angels fly and heaven preserves us, I will always be your angel and the true rank of my place amongst men is that I will carve out a future with my two bare hands of fire and flint. Enough to learn to fly high amongst this valley, with the wind, feeding like a vulture on the mill and giving my expertise to the rusting leviathan and forest torn town.

The forest is my solace, the gardens my turf, the river my rest and the hills my lust. The bush telegraph, the grapevine can discover many things about Velouria. I aim to win your trust, your friendship, your emotions, to keep you grounded but with your sights set upon the perfect nature of your work. The composure of a comet. I bow to your mischievous, heartfelt touch and silky-smooth demeanour, your wilder humour and energy, your smile, your graceful pure smile; your sense of sensibleness. Your jaunty yet serious brown eyes. A natural sweet cherished mother of milky moon drenched castles in my mind. A beauty I would always miss with these eyes before.

In lavender it remains
As forlorn hope and pungent strain
In the monkish flower garden
The majestic old rose
Wait on tea trolleys to be consumed
Yet the thorn its pinprick blood delays the storm
In a teacup
Our love like that rose
Blooming.

I decided to dwell on those aspects I have pride in. Our meeting ranks so highly in these. The pervading air of contentment of your memory, the cutoff points our love resounds in me still. I have a friend in you of that, I am sure. That knowing smile. The tenderness I have viewed through the viewfinder of our relationship and stood firm against the struggle we have been through. Sometimes I view life through my daughter's eyes and try to be worthy. I love her so and I can hardly deal with the pain of not seeing her, holding her and being close to her. It is such a sad state of affairs when one is not able to stem the flood of instinct.

It could be beautiful. Cherished destiny led us wonderfully feathered to inspire this to happen. Sweet beauty, compassion, devotion, will and desire is what companionship is about. Meaningful fulfilment and astonishing links have been forged. When you look in the whirlpool the form and dynamics are a healthy heartbeat of our relationship. On my own for far too long that is all. Have faith in us and I will show you a world full of promise, a feeling with sentiment-centred saved soul, a serious lament from will's mystery, a clarity, clear and true, a care to wipe the slings and arrows from your heart and a pleasure to climb the stairs of your dreams. Our dreams are dear; our past intertwined our daughter beautiful and our futures together. Cowgirl in the sand I can feel our presence through the walls of your tower. No man loves like I love you, delightful and clear like the steps to heaven, crazy you had been, enjoying solitude like the well of the damned, closest often seen in the bluebell array in its heyday, in the lines of a statue in the heraldry of the tunes you sang, hungry like the ghosts that listen at the lantern. Hear me calling! Let me dispel any fearful motion from your courteous compassion; braver, more honourable soul than my agreeable self.

The present I forget is in the limelight I try, to bind my emetic loneliness with processional rest of spirit and guidance which flowers through me like strength which brings the beauty alive. To see the world with peaceful comprehension, and the shapes and images of understanding, transforming even the bird on the wing to such ability and truth for a creative touch ultimately to be a positive influence on her mind through deed and thought. Distraught with relativity in this the caring minute of recent time I see the world though her eyes. It could be beautiful cherished destiny led as wonderfully feathered to inspirations happenings of sweet beauty that atoned stranger than talent, fascinated devotion and soothed closer than compassion where serious desire wantonly reigns in fulfilment like a rider upon a ground of ability to transpose form and dynamics from instinctive vantage to parallel your souls touch:

I draw you in
A smile of plenty and eyes that rise
The spark that cries between the sighs
And magic moments
-a chance
Beam from up high.
We lance my fears
And parole my role
External droll remarks
Cool sensed truths and twitter
Of fatherhood
Mirror glances of fate beams
I borrow whiles
In an expanse of happiness
Forked and gulfed from my control
Parallels my void mass
A minor image

Suddenly

Love and Green

Michael

The lighthouse fans the reckless sea. The scene is thus set. Ele'hail her ivory love in a tower impregnable. Guarded by dragons, fools, jesters, butterflies, dragonflies, were-wolves and bats. Her vicissitudes are extinguished by her body, white resplendent, and your pulsating touch, fringed by honesty's gesture, small and figurative amongst the darkness is your swan white body -is this your wondrous smile? To cartelise windows to our soul reminds my fingers I have once optimised your loving arms. Solace drips into my heart like a pinhole to ride a white pony into the waves and breathe in air inside my cuteness bracken blown dancing tune; a conical smile for a digging stone of my heart's principle. Chances ambulant fly. As chance would have it, he received a reply via a dove on the wing.

Hid under a spreading mortal hazel-chestnut cave Michael sat, light sheets of shadowy rain falling down in a realm of coquettishness. Since the dove was all that is left embroidered gently in the breeze it appeared above spiral puddles, the wood like old heads so tired of everything, yet with the billets glistening and Lenore scared at what tomorrow brings, the ark slips in the rain. Hemmed in by a circle of saplings the dove dropped into the circle of his camp.

He watched as his hands sprung to capture the dove in flight. As it grew in his hands the eyes flicker and plunge into their darkness a breath to prise open his fingers and his prayers, hot, sweet and cherry kind are martyred. His good aspirations tingle, yet its beak is poised ubiquitous. The nobler velour of the sheet-white host is a gazing of star-sweeping nirvana as he reached to hold her. "My face alights on you so close, yet logic lights the minim rays that there is no-one." Yet the dove's pulse races. The dove there in my palm. No wind moans my coming, no greater love among the company of wolves which howl. I search for a place amongst the reeds yet as his breast was held open its beak sank deep beneath. Memory flicks and flutters like a dove over the lake of hopes, flap and circle over the crazy tree stumps of my heart's desire. The letter's uncertainties have wishes revolving in its wings aglow. I missed you before you had gone. She spoke to this dove a magical madrigal to send it on its way: "Let honesty fly through this English sky do not stone this dove for its love is ours, black out the summer sky do for its beauty is not yours, hide the strawberries and cream for their taste is not yours. Let not the storm of life knock it from its flight. Loves honesty flies and cries the sound from its throat loves first cut healed like a lump in the throat no longer to be feared never to be stolen from the kiss which is always kinder than fiction. But only love can break your heart.

**Chapt. 3 Chrysalinity**

Michael returned to the fire. The wasted figure of a man stood over the embers of a fire. The quarry of the hunt had not been caught, not been brought down by courage in those wastes of ice and snow. More realistically it had not been brought back to those who converted the beast. A gathered throng had greeted the empty proud hunting party this evening. The embers were all that was left of their hope, their grievances, and their dreams. The power of the beast inside Amaeigin was palpable.

The dove flew overhead, spread-eagled against the sky. I didn't mean to. Michael closed his eyes. Some part of him was glad. Inside, but the latter-day-angelic-kiss had been wiped off of his lips forever. Remorse gripped his lips and made him pucker and blow the embers, sparking and winking burned the corner of the letter. He stroked his bristles as he read the remnants- "Our talisman will always be peace on the wing." He thought of the symbols of responsibility and unfurled a determination that lay inside his dormant mind.

The living earth goddess sheltered his thoughts and she spoke- "thank you for still loving me though I do not deserve your words. Determine your soul that searches rightful discerning compassion for your child and your salvation." A spark rested on his arm and it followed timelines of frenetic pathos, and winsome closeness. The spark of constant memory is a demand for the truth and mystery, the opposite to sods law –a universal constant of the substitution principle of the universe- contained within the living earth goddess's words. Her halo of honesty flies in the face of uncertainty. She would buy harmony, peace and resolution for there is to be no more pain. The spirit of creativity, fantasy and inspiration of the living proof danced in the trees without cautioning us to be careful, realistic, or to remember the limitations of being human.

Her unlimited, discerning nature encased within her cocoon left him by the lake of beauty, strength and virtue. The light from the shimmering sun dwindled as he stepped to its bank. Its bank was the resilience that she had told him of. She began like the opening of transcendental music. She spoke lines of such delights. His resolve wavered and Velouria's plot thickened. No audience had she, no woes, no objections. His heart leapt and raced as stories unfolded of such delicious, delicate demure abandon, such scurrilous happenings he had only thought of as his anticipation of his wants. His awe shored up the passion of her figurative nature caught up in a grip of euphoria. She surpassed his fantasy and gave him some he had never wanted, nor thought possible. Such a future butterfly was she, so brave, so wilful, so wonderful, and so arousing yet encased within her pupae prison.

His flame walked around the shore, behind and burning in appreciation for her glory. The glory let him understand the true nature of a butterfly. Her delicate poignant powerful vitriolic majestic voice stood out from the dark to his ears, ears deaf from crying, the shadows of her ghost on his tongue the shimmering of her heat under skin, dustless as the virtue that composed her. Compassion dripped from every fibre of his being as a rhapsody played in his ears:

"Thou art the star to light my way, turning my path from night to day. Thou art my joy, my grief, my sorrow, my hope of grace today tomorrow. Thine is the power and can relieve all fears and bring me lasting peace. Peace comes from there and joy wending quiet repose all else transcending. Crowned by thy love then life has meaning, thy shining glance thy soul revealing with courage high I raise again triumphant in a world of pain. Thou art the star to light my way turning path from night to day."

Often in this life you will be. With chrysalinity your thoughts go, but we shall would. With Velouria I would always. With Ele'hail I would always. Out of snow she dings, acting from melody she swings in this would adore. Together you linger but I like the cold west wind linger also, like collywobbles before a play, like a haze in the bay, like we would, not may. Ash Wednesday. I have decided to light a candle in the church. There would be something in this religion thing. One never knows for sure.

Many great deeds have your mother done I was part to many and heard enough to keep me in well clamour, honour, compassion. I for my part swung these around like a moose, its antlers in the air, tracing moonglow patterns in the mist. My, she is a redeemer. My she is a champion of champions. Back in the days of drinking she would have to peel me off the ceiling in adoration of her. A fine woman. She gave us so much Ele'hail. She gave of her soul, her body but she unravelled. I forsook the challenge and rested. Resided with my ghosts for far too long, controlled by others. I was Mr Nobody Knows.

Mr nobody knows is a friend to doggies, in the rain and in the shine. Owners' roses dart as he snatches and they bound as he catches up on sleep. From the oak tree you can spy him as he searches and winds his belt on a branch to climb. Mr nobody knows swears in the grass, passes out in the church, gives pennies to the guy in exchange for wealth. Mr nobody knows is a stayer in the park, a swinger after dark, a listener in the silence, a poacher in the distance. He knows the rabbit caressed wood and nasty boys with all their toys to steal, with a handful of hair and muddy worms he makes potions in the pubs.

Mr nobody knows is a person everybody knows but he doesn't know that Mr nobody knows. Mr nobody knows is a person he knows only far too well, a drinker from the well, smell, dell, bell. His only art is his chant. Nobody knows like nobody knows. He is the man who claps the failure. He is the man who delights in regalia. He is nerve gas factory in the house that jack built. He has bricks in his mind and builds a house in every woman he sees. He carries his water in a crisp packet to empty over the gollywogs head of steam. He puts the polos wildly in the stream. He licks the cars clean. He does nothing in between his actor's dream. He is the murmuring train in the rain. He comes to your birthday party to hear you scream. He comes to your letterbox to plant a seed at your door. He likens best when he dreams of all the clothes he possessed as a teen. He is always there, a vision in the mist, water on the dish, a writer after dusk. He throws thoughts to the birds and looks after Mrs nobody knows who never was, never is but in his hair, he keeps her. Like a ship. Like the lipstick he saw on the glass. Like the fantasy of three dogs chasing him in the meadow he only wants to sit upon not park.

Mr nobody knows is a cleaner after dark, a line painter, a gardener, a taxi-driver, and a plasterer. He could have been anything. He is no one in particular. He is indefinitely present in writing down your particulars. He is a particle of physical peculiar menace that lives on a council estate and drives a zero into walls. He has a cabined ear he uses to fear the phantoms he chases. He has a pyramidal eye he uses to say *goodbye*. This is the only word he knows and you will hear his bellow loud and bold. "*Goodbye*, miss, *goodbye*."

Trouble is he never goes Mr nobody knows. He is there and in his car he is here. He is in July a ghost, in august an ill wind, in September a mouse and in October a king of fools, a joker, and a porter. He always says sorry. He will right your laughter but he will never teach you how to write your chords. He would never be told as if to say a word of history. He never tells you anything Mr nobody knows!

In November he is a bonfire guy, who lives in a mad mad town, who rides a mad horse madly. He is a multi-coloured swap shop at daybreak and a tailgate light at dusk. He lives in a birdcage with hatpins for food. He collides with clouds as he goes too far; he looks at broken hearts under the microscope but is always peeking at the sickening sadness in her eyes while drinking Spanish plonk at the flamenco club. Though he's always at home. Ham-fisted with energy he rides his motorbike over stepping-stones when he should have jumped, but flicks and twists his *goodbye* anyway. For Mr nobody knows has not a second to spare to wish you happiness in the snow. Ele'hail does not need Mr nobody knows for you see in December he is a snowman. He will melt your food in front of you if you say hello. Then say I've had more hot dinners than you have ever known. So, leave him be, leave him cold. Leave him outside in the snow. He will only say *goodbye* if you don't say "hello!" "No!" Mr nobody knows, "No hello!" That nobody knows.

But my loyalty was only ever to her. I think far off. In another planetary, gadgetry, plaintiff role her heart unravelled. I bailed out. I forsook her kindness to this world of would. She is wonderful, wonderful like a butterfly stuck in her pupal stage:

Most men will worship
Front room dreams of you
The snap of the hose
As a shaft of light from heaven
Speaking from beyond the grave
God's easy night

Soldiers and fathers
Sweet professional flaws
A crane's switching glance
And flick of fin
Dance neath robes of white
God's easy night

The moment my head hits the pillow
Trying to be a poltergeist
A dreamer
Like the sound of babble brook
I keep close to you

### God's easy night

Purple fairy wings aglow
On a plain and forest patch
The resin from my eyes
Cover my elegant passion
As I slip into your bed or something
God's easy night

I hear your bequests
For this butterfly I have lost
Escaped from the net of my heart
I am willing but not able
To come this way
God's easy night

Taken aback a bit. The highlights of my life as I lay them out here are not exactly what you may think splendid. The lowlifes are all around me still crawling from bridge to post and occupying spaces the rocks should cover. The Billy goat in my life has a bigger uncle. They both crave the greener grass. Hopefully this will meld with this story. A story with subplots and Jacobs ladders of subtle practiced webs of receipt. Like the wolves which grace your room I am the hunter of all the strange, the interpreted range of tomorrow's wishes and today's regrets. Well, your candour is my order, your features my armour, yours the chance that maybe you would, though in my dreams I would pick you up and swing you round and tell you how adorable. I would in my world of wouldness. If I think you would quench your thirst on my words then I have achieved the unachievable. To love you. That which is achievable as he light by which we achieve greatness. That our union brought such a splendid girl such as you into this world is the story of chrysalinity.

I have just spent a week of cocooned pain. It is just such a short word for slightness, a deep-felt fascination and horror. A preoccupation with those aspects which do one harm. Recoiling in self-fascination. A delirium where one does not know who one is. Do you dig what I mean? You can give all to a woman. You can take everything but this is never enough. My love lies in a chrysalis; a woman cruel I know this but I shall resurrect it here on these pages; streamlined pages of love from me to you:

> The caterpillar crawls
> And that is all
> Crawls and eats and that is all
> The delicate whiles the purloined lines
> Of listened chastened bed flow
> Stretch to occasion and grow
> And lie beneath haze green beige
> The colours of chameleon
> Dusted trusted loins splinter
> A recoiled sinister growl
> So, each delicate line is misted
> Like wood.
> And a butterfly descending from
> Its song

On the open harbourfront of afternoons sometimes both would sit and in each other there was a dreamlike plainness and excitement which they drew upon for strength and triumph and trust. Many an hour pressed like specks of light between their lips as they kissed dreaming of your wondrous form. But drawn, in awe and wonder to the senses of one another. Oh, longing, oh joy, oh still my beating heart to try to make each moment stop passing and hang in suspended animation like a work of art. Blissful and eventful their lives circled around each other's mutual trust and respect. Thoughtful and creative they both achieved and one night sought an angel orchestrated from both the control of passing destiny and their own feelings. It was reality that plucked you from the sea angels and demons and gods and sirens. She washed your hands and continued to teach. Angel' rain taught what I choose never to forget, though, in the Helter-skelter preposterousness of ordinarily she saw it as wasted youth, disrespect for responsibility.

In their words, their speech, their love- a butterfly is coming she said. Common ground with the buttercups was all he found, too high too happy too exulted to play his part he would not accept that it could happen to him. Vast dust accessed their ways and grew to change its shape in their relationship while she matured as the apple by her side, and out of this nothingness a separation sprung. But Velouria was clever and wise to keep the angel secret and healthy. Michael for his own merit kept her will alive in everything he said did or thought. For he loved her dearly.

Velouria would not believe this. She thought he had betrayed her the sea demons whispered to her in her loneliness. Her heart unravelled. As an angel promise the wicked winds parted the two and as with all mortals they sacrificed each other for the brave, determined, sweet love that is Ele'hail and the wind that had called her back to the sea ceased and was calm. It had wreaked its havoc and claimed its figure of loneliness, forever searching wondering inspired and tortured. The tower loomed in the dark brooding sky, hopelessness in ice and stone.

Every night the angel called and sent calm and every chord spoke of passion answering endeavour and peace so that the two, though apart would never be unhappy again. "As sure as my mind is an entity so will her wings never flop and the angelic passion it doesn't fade just like the jumper, she packed you in from this island. I send my light out to you every night to keep you from the chocolate of misnomer: My thoughts to the ocean go swinging sweet majestic gull flies upon wing neath innocent flow. Bring me the answer in a baby's moon-beam bitter-sweet chocolate melted secrets, happy harbour resplendent glow, scattering light into my dark night that spans the crest of a wave. Sentiment from angels comes towards this familiar shore. My thoughts to ocean keep; enlightening quintessential silent deep fear neath innocence seep. My wishes beam upon the tide, walk upon goodness I weep, this whip of dreams embarks and I wonder at your sense and goodness; cleverness that spans the crest of a wave. For lonely are we, sweeping and gliding joyous trust inquisitive, in feathers of yesterday's gathering as she devours the horizon for a piece of chocolate. For distance doesn't care."

Extract from journal ad 605: As the mist closes in, sitting here in pale Miserable light, reminds me, mermaids me of the saltmarsh-sea-specked-peppercorn below me like resolve in my mind, the dogs chase and harry the pale moonlight. I remember what the little girl said "You must be lonely" and the joy of recognition spread like sea shanties to a future unclouded by my aching heart, my generation. The consoled North Sea, pushes for jolly pale slime and shake and hook. A lung-lapped seagull soars and swells its raffle high in the sky made of flying whiles. Ceaseless waves are aware to swell and are gone.

The half-moon beckons and already I am over that moon. I will get to see you, my dove, my purple fairy winged sparkles. Of that I am determined. That you are in this world I dared to, I held my breath to, and I thank the skies and zephyrs of the four winds. I scarce dream lest I am taken by currents way out to sea-breathing coastline beckoning and in walking into the storm to bring you a sprig of the finest pearl coated shells from oh some old mermaid's purse. I rang to the joyful and the joyous rang out. I sprang to the hopeful and the frenetic warbling sang out. The spring is here I hear Velouria murmur in her sleep and I bless the dew dawning sun upon her face, such beauty wandering there closed and full in her soul like the buddings of new life. As she casts a wilful look in your direction, I can only beam at her from my hideaway in the woods. Moon at her from the depths of the tree canopy; smile an inner smile to her wondrous nature.

I mean five months old and you already mean more to me than my feet which mean a hell of a lot to a man actually. Therein the feet maketh the man and all that. I mean cut a piece of myself and grew by my side. I bet you are thinking I wish he could have been there to watch over me. We have always been me and your guardian angel. You will always have a guardian angel looking after you wherever you come or go whether you rest or low or in high places dwell. I do not give up on constancy, rather engulf her as my own for only in concern I hereby decree love, honesty and ability that I so much regret you, though wish you, pupability.

If I could flex a muscle for every time I have kept your image precious through this world of men. It is not necessarily the easiest but I would have settled down and been your daddy if they had let me. A fugitive a damn dog on his way deep down south on a hiding to nothing followed by deputy rankling and separated dastardly mutts all in drag and shouting obscenities. How? My spirit guide wanders in a forest full of dreams a place we can explore. I implore you that it was not that spirit was lacking. I will become your servant. They just wouldn't let me. Enough already. T'is constancy I adore.

To give up on your mother is not something I wanted. I know she was the best woman I could ever imagine. Just to look at her pictures makes me feel how right she was. She never made decisions rashly. I have to fulfil my side of the bargain that is all. I still think I can have a good role to play in your life. I know that reasoned decisions will be made. Velouria was so much my support. She was my joy, my sustenance, mighty confidant. Now I have her formula under my skin, in my heart, on my mind. She was so gifted, more of a woman I could never and will never see. As you know only too well. I think that all I want to do is to provide for you. I hope you take this gesture the right way. All I really want is to be non-frivolous, hardworking; astute. I only hope it is not too late. Sometimes I would give up on this happy-go-lucky lifestyle and formulate plans.

I have the right on my side. I have the ability to make myself count in this world of would, I am sure. Though not for its own sake rather to shoot the moon. I require guidance. I require the ability to go out and get 'em.

I think you have picked Mr nobody knows. He looks at the jetsam the gently woven material in his wasteland and hand to mouth eats the dead seaweed to amount to sustenance. Not much doing; not much trying. Just beach combing. The waves out on the sea show flashes of other people's lives, some marvellous some mundane, a smile an odd remark is collected as it cascades upon the beach but always a compliment, always a gesture from the muse who should seek waves to break onto the surf and collapse after having shown so much promise. For the heads that bob up and down after the undertow are yours but rooted to my feeling their suspense, feeling their force but am stuck on this side of the wave too nervous to flounder amongst them. I play it safe and wander lonely as a cunt amongst the shell remains and seaweed trails of life's deposited fragments, I wish to hear the heartbeat of the sea, want to be pulled under and struggle to survive neath the currents which pull at my legs, no promise of this which I will gain, no promise of this which I try in vain to stop reaching desolate on the shore.

Michael stood at the foot of the tower. He had breached security. True, full dappled sunshine sparkles where once barren soil was. Crowfeet on Martello stairs as the name of the rose, fleeing in a summer's sky, brashness for boots and tears for goodbyes. The more or less a patient Michael winged his lust from toe to toe and continued to climb. The crows cawed a warning.

"They are lovely creatures" he thought, "but they are not to fault"- charman of oak wood, celestially spiralling his water in Eden, cloaked and hidden from the soldiers' view he had collected some tea to Velouria's tower and saw the baby Ele'hail in her crib and streaked his eyes with Velouria's. Not so much intimate, but a flood of memories descended like the stairs he eventually had to disappear down. So, solace-weaving, bosom-heavingly good he stood apart the clouds to watch her face, a face of elegance and ripe-berried specialness and awe, struck seven times wonder in a face so fair of grace and expansive in its prettiness. Yet he was jostled by the guards out of the tower. The bear roar collapses on the beach and its undertow reveals the shells while wiping the words I love you from his lips.

Love larks shall link hands neath yesterday's light, lantern shining in the dusk, proceeding through the cautious hush with bushel grazing beneath a desolate white the jolly game the evening spill hark with voices clear and shrill of childhood laughter and constancy shown glinting gathering snow for a snowy throne upon crushing frosted lake of need, an icicle decorates her trusty swan. I love her majesty so- such joy of beauty breaths a dynamic measure; eyes rally Egremont's treasure with pods of steel and familiarity: the lake of tears and purity. I beheld in my guise the cygnet not to love in vain last summer with borrowed love and pleasure for without a word she spells my angel's endeavour to bless, constancy in my duress. The swan's white body cartilage windows to the soul bracken-blown reed-hidden mystery downy feathers that fear beauty principles come from its beak nearest to an ambulant squeak. Precious neath wings of her mother, chest of silver neath halo of gold the cygnet borne in glory, the space between her cabined ears bodes farethewell my dears as she hides her secret love. The bread in our hands her winter reed, the landscape of ice pale and wan beneath her wings exposes the jollity of cold red noses where foxes bask all summer long, nuzzled close to your song. A baby's open surprise depends upon love like a flurry of snow descends neath wonton sky we peck and peer at wishes falling far and near with sublime chill I chance my hand into white dust a snowballs demand. But where to throw? At piety or honour the letting go- phizz-whizz into the drift land on where dreams rift.

Maybe like the lapwing nestled dear she slumbers on hearts and flowers to keep me from wanting another night. Another night. Wrestled in the removed strings of a dream, crested as a wave from beyond the grave, I sit in conjecture and simplicity. For I will listen to constancy's heartbeat rise and fall, of all your own my angel. For from up above you rest, from sequinned sweated brow you present, all my labours hour sent to a sequinned pulse a trace to be. To be by your side like warmth or glad tiding brings a hope to you all goodness springs, in hearty smile and delicate giggle I pour a cup of designated twiddle and look upon your upturned eyes closer to heaven than wings which beat beyond the skies and make a prayer to Jesus thus day shall bring me closer to constancy and let honour sing a colonnade of roses for to bless your humungous innocence and happiness around these shores in weeks or days or hours to hold your sweet body and make this time ours.

Yet as I descended the steps I was unable to hide from my mind's eye as I followed the trace of your hairline and follow the rise and fall of your breath, that I long to see you again. The burnt offerings of yet another wooded relinquished potion to heterogenic waves of conversation- the stairs of the tower in prospect under the lure of love leeward seeping slow dive requisite tenderness. Please, please let me get what I want this time. Happiness is what you bring, I am swelled with pride and gladness and can smell your babyness in my nostrils, and near my beating heart I hold a limp flower for you that has been adorning this casket of sorrow. I am ashamed to have let myself wallow in this manic self-pity. No longer my dear.

I wish to make you proud of me, as, or rather somewhat like the pride I hold in you. I could beat wild oceans into a puddle for you to step, ring nettled undergrowth to point the beauty of that which lies and bunny flops beneath, afford the largest stem into the raging torrent of my heart, leap small haystacks at a single bound to find the white rabbit nestling beneath blankets of soft eiderdown all asleep next to mummy's angelic gown. I want to deepen the felt touch of your clothes, whiten the gleam of talcum powder on your toes pray to widen your smile at my behest; perhaps awaken a youthful dewdrop of interest. Formulate great plans and follow them through for constancy. I want to make you happy like me you do. This Easter I will pray to you in the gutted ramshackle church where we made our vows, took succour and wished for you:

A glassy goodnight

In sleepy held arms
Lost to heaven but close to lace
The sugar plum fairy charms
Her smile to gather apace
And find holy berry
Her ace a fond embrace
Grace true loves trace
Pleasures to bury
Upon Ele'hail's face
Renewed hope and happiness
Her thoughts perchance to race
Glad tidings to her caress
Qu'est-ce tu fais
Paperchase

## Chapt. 4 Substitution Principle

I think Amaeigin is overstepping his authority. All is not well in Velouria's house. Many times, must he have waited to have them done for; soft spoken calm of her threat like a caterpillar gently brushing his skin. Did she learn like a caterpillar that it cannot fly till open-winged calls its name, from its purposed depths of considered pondering? Consolidated Velouria will wait in the chrysalis for its wings to unfurl. His evil craft a beat of thick blood beckoning low and soft to trick her into emerging in a showy gravel drained period. Your mother looked into my soul and found only a pale reminder of what could be, too fond of my own security, too bashful for what lies in my way? The candle flickers and gives over the sense of wonder I have found in you. Need I say that I doubt. Simply that, that Amaeigin may have a sinister motive for keeping you in this pupal stage.

It was busy and not nice brother. My daddy was a rubber bullet in the hell of make believe, gruelling around the sheen, capered up around the trails, the pink assurance parted four arrogances manifested in a drive of tyceralene with taboo marked on it; a stiff upper hand. I needed a helping hand so I ran into the past but in the nightingale of the night, a symbol of attack or help, the bullet may have soft edges but roams the catalyst in the small of pain. We want to label failure so I whirl and fire at the phantoms and sincere desire reins the moon face cos I knew how long it'd last like wit on board our glistening trail a spear to lance the wound. Find me by your secret stream, the fountain of hysteria.

I doubt if I have the strength to devise a way forward, I am sick of the compromise for in my heart I know that I have a deal to offer, a dedication to give, a role to play. I crave neither support nor friendship. Just a way out of here to help her, a way to expand and grow so that she does not feel so wretched, so bemused, so predestined to fail. As a caterpillar and a caterpillar can crawl and eat, that is all. Oh, for wings to pull her free in quantity that would have documented the total quality of a moment. The headway of the oneness united with the air would be like a visible song. How are you in the caterpillar house?

At night I hear your crying from my perch at the foot of the tower. I am drawn towards the castle gates to hear you Ele'hail with my shore-footed light:

I sense in your screams a truth
That forms on your mouth but was never given
If you love me so, why are you missing?
I answer because you are an angel
You sigh it's an illusion
I sense in your dreams an accusation
That seeps from my pages to an open book
When you love me so why do you wait?
I consider back I'm already there
You scream "where exactly daddy?"
I sense in your means a wanting
That comes like the sap rising in my veins
If you love me, why don't you give?
I answer I have never stopped
You scream more
I sense in your anger a forgiveness
That flickers with alternatives and understanding

# THE CHRYSALIS TIME

If you love me so, are you going to be there?
I answer your screams with hope
The meaning of the word yes

The moon-beguiled peppered star-sweltered sky was limited only by the pale eyelid glance from the moonglow bright. I have gone to the witch in the forest to change my appearance to an old woman. The dubiousness of my form swept away like the seaweed on a tide, spider crabs rushing to the shore foraging so high so that its orbit is their ambition. For flotsam I weave my wave and angels swoon at its glory and mouth the haze of a gaze. The feeling speaks the truth. A forced florid taste sensation of my future haunts the coast and my ears float languidly onto the mighty breakwater flung from joy-lidded feeling so alive. My purpose is to disguise myself and enter the tower, your tendrils in my arms a star fish meets my acquaintance and the treasure is found. Happy precious portrait of Ele'hail that I can really love. I am to be an old woman.

The purple faeries shook a panacea of powder over the field and the children played. The dance of the pipes was heard above the shrill pleasant sounds of the witch's theory was explained to Michael. The quills shivered in the mist, the purple fairy queen beamed a warm sunshine heaven over the field, not far from the sea. Near to far the shining grass quivered in the sea breeze. Guilty footfalls winded vainly over the vegetation as Michael's youth hidden left the field. An orchard fairy left his magic apple by the shore and Michael stooped to pick it up. As he took a bite the faeries were shown to them. They flew and darted away from each other and formed gateways into the secret ways he had forfeited. A man finished by his walk the slowness of light and sound wandered in his memories and the sea declared its jubilation upon reaching the fairy shire. The deliverance of night closed in. The pink moon was on its majestic way and broke the seal of space that meant so much to the man. Some sheltered by the brook whispering. Michael could hear them and as a fairy feigned death, she waved her hand to catch the fairy dust that spiralled from their wings. This fairy quenched her dreams' lost secret to be kept with her blossomed smile back in the world of dens and pubs and cafes.

They whispered the secret of what was between the sand and the sea. It is the little piece of regret's reminiscences which docks in a pale moonlight's ripples. It is the work tools of a cobbler working late at night. It is the longing for a prince to come. It is the forgotten dreams of a little girl who has what she needs; it is the tragedy of wanting a dreaming man. It is the treasure of a thousand shipwrecks. It is the loneliest sound, the silence between the waves; it is a rivers shale flame and a soldier's shame, a whale's game. It is the difference between being and reality, the difference between coasting and frivolity, between the cake and the mix, the art and the fixer, the joy and the delicious, the light and the dark the snow in the park. At evening it is the last show at dusk as it is the creeping shadow. In the morning it is the joy of the nearing day said in a way that a prostitute keeps wrath. The sorrow's moth. The sacred cloth. The fairies were there in the forest watching Michael secretly. They began to dance around the spiral tree singing:

Up the spiral tree quests
Spiders moss at times behest
At Halloween mark the ladder up
At its base a golden cup
Ray me far so la tee doe
Forward the spiral tree commands
Its metal army to seek demands
From its raging flare
A spiral to its lair
Ray me far so la tee doe
The faeries dance amongst the beech
Its shadows covert for to reach
The sunlit dappled canopy
Of which witches rare and floppy…
Ray me far so la tee doe
Desire and cynem give to the swan
Of the squirrel's winged alarum
Tiny wings unfurled aglow
To continue this house of doe
Ray me far so la tee doe

As Michael sat in the woods, he was first aware of tiredness in him. A squirrel ran around the forest clearing shrilly squeaking "chip chip chip" (roughly translated that it was greener there), a lament only to those who redeem themselves. Like the dogs which scooted and frolicked in his territory as the fir tree lurched from side to side in the breeze. Dandelion breath, neath the pretty bows swaths of memories rustle the red and yellowing phantoms twirl and laugh at me in my dreams. Only figments, pigments of my soul; a soul facing up to reality my Velourias brevity to find seeds scattering over Woodbury hollow. Cross-looming slender forms. The mushroom crushed by flowing gaze risking losing to slip into Pascal's dew to sink to its knees in pity for Boudicca to quicken my hand to grant me this. For long have I held study? To rub the feverish toil under the dying sun of summer sought the magpie's wing, the elephant's sting, this squirrel's silly prance too harsh for this art. For a new life. The hollow he chose was like a slingshot nest. It was where all the cheeky fathers pretended to be trolls to their sons. Yet daughters are fairer. Daughters are daring and wise. Clever and sharp to the open frontages and harbour doors made from the very trees the bees bury their honey in. It was by a stream that I will change, he thought.

Ele'hail peaceful and new, rather like the deer that chastened my view amidst the language of play and decay swaying majestically twixt stream and bank the rocking cradle I await. Holy and bright, safe and clean knowing mortalities flight. I long to cradle both in my arms. Hollow time invests the crows' call. To water the running stream glanceless as the sky than the pond than the puddles in your mind. Now letting children into their secrets is what a squirrel's life is all about. Like the one who lives at Waltham abbey where the naughty boys throw chips at each other and pretend to be King Harold, but if you listen the squirrel will tell you where he got his voice. One in the eye for the naughty boys "chip chip chip".

There was a lazy whispering to the leaves which folded like the rain and sprang into life. On slindays the squirrel is always busy. The squirrel does not sit on the fence and he saves his memory for fruitless incessant searching "Pookah Pookah Poojabby!" went the jay as he rustled past her nest. Being admirable in wing and colour she thought herself very grand but in actual fact spent all her time avoiding people- she was so gay she had to. The squirrel and the jay were fine friends. One wouldn't want to be seen by just anyone would one!

A place of calm, serenity, niceness. A place where save means secure appears Baldwin's Pond. Yet like bubbles they blow are yet to see the light of loneliness and heirlooms of day and joy in its coming. The pope log as luminosity folds its hard clenched hands and leeches upon the soil with sands pointing a communion with the liberal chimneys. "Pip Pip Pip" went the paddling geese on their way to the pond. Try saying anything else when you've been flying all the way from Canada. All things are natural said the forest wind as Michael continued his journey along the stream of Woodbury hollow to Baldwin's Pond.

I sold my soul to the witch and in return she changed my form. Trinkets and gaskets took the form of the vendor. All shapes and sizes all colours and matches. There was so much to choose from, so many ringlets to purchase, so much sex to drive. A neon smile held the pulse. The pulse that each child missed, the missing deterioration of the heart. The silence of the lambs. The gait of the long-legged bait. There were cathedrals and wells for hire. Women to bed upon, lions to run from. Yet the last moment was a heartbeat, as he drank the phial of liquid the witch had given him. So pure. So, energising. So restful:

> Sometimes I have not the climes
> To make the wind moan
> Or call your mother on the phone

But lost is all I ever am
My lonely sweet marked pen
My only home
But time it flies
Philandering in pale vagaries
In times of trouble, you may be lost
In times of fortune pay the cost
Yet together in reflection
We will be chances cloud
A moment cherished is never tossed
But time it flies
Though friends be few
And loves wages high
In tune and security and a lie
A stitch or line in a minor key
Will beliefs chagrin rise
Upon your face, like this July
But time it flies
Your birth I cry and visit here
Carve your name my life to gain
A steady course on a windswept plain
Neath grassy sky I lay me down
My path seems so fortunate
To your mother's door again.
But time it flies.

Yet hope and clarity are here with me to be a forest prayer neath jet and amber find a deer's heart in his leafy pond I do not interpret but feel all the same as a writer of rabbit-trap-fictions that baldies do not get the ichthus with their crumpled old dollars, trying to rid me of my bones tortured by these riches that won't love me nor let me go. She switched my form. All the hope in the world budged that stream. No, the river keeps on going the same. Trusting morals, lasting treats, the beckoned neonatal seconded his pillow of sand in the middle of the night and the pleasure was everlasting. This the faeries knew time passed on until Michael was an old woman, knurled and wizened, old and fruitless. He was an old woman scrapped from his skin. He lay on the floor gasping. His wizened frame got up and his stretched skin breathed. He had emerged.

Michael had one last wish wrestled from the witch's spell. Michael was to visit Merlin's cave to shapeshift and spend one last night in his lover's arms. Michael, from a hideout in the oak, the mythical ways he thought to momentarily change from the old woman's guise to his own form, wearing skin he wore. He had swelled you on his patience your taste. Honey as he woke up, he left you. Childe born. I lend you my ear my wishes circles that hit the coast. Circles that come too near, too far away. I leave me on your doorstep and walk the cliff. The swell the birds. I cannot go. I am here for eternity. Wearing his tattoos. Pinnacles of rockpersuade of what captivated your constancy. Heartbroken I let close the tide held in my hands. I let the wind caress as once angel rain's hands used to. The craft sways neath the soft vegetation on the cliff face. What traces in your arms? What you don't know. Circles in the oak hideout. Nothing is good enough for you.

Throw caution to the wind. In footfall Michael scales the cliff edge to an egg; He picks it up in the structure of the key. In the nothing of weather and grievance. I only miss you so. Strain another sail in and circle the coast. So pure, so amazing. So restful, my sympathy in the pulse of that egg. Its heartbeat sounded on her pillow in the middle of the night. Merlin's cave give me back my daughter! Swimming against your word, intentions against the tide. I falter, I shelter. I riddle my way out of the bravest happiness where the coven runs, spinning in the wind. The moth of my reputation goes beyond regret beyond the icy waters beneath. Like a mouth in the foot in the face. Like rivulets of sweat on your brow. Yet I free my kin in the bird. Searching for the answer I see you. I love you, Velouria. I lend my words to the water and entangle my hair in the salty air. I nest neath the cliff point. The hollow golden hair of the spider's coven. Yearning for Angel' rain. These points of light. Her soft skin on her back. Her feet, her clenched breed of honesty. A message for the heart. To sleep with you for one night. To fight the good fight. To summon your wants till morning light. To understand the mind, to find you fading and in glory. Our daughter lonely in the cot of the beach beckons us; our pines of threads come to meet the rivers of honesty to atone the mystical mountains. The egg key of renewal. Castles are distant in my breast. My face is good. I take on his form. I am let into her room and talk to her sweetly. She offers her arm. I lean. I love in my arms so sweet to send. She opens her arms and I am engulfed.

Michael woke up on the cliff, the salty air mingled with his wizened form. He looked into a pool of water. His face was weathered and old, his clothes a musty grey and beneath the wasted form of an old woman. He knew he had one place to go. The stone circle. To cement his form. To remain like this, till the time came to reveal himself. The henge loomed into the present. Shadows of creation, shade from pillars of rock, smiles of conservation stakes to plant the runes. Hardness and harmony. Pensive and hollow he approached them becoming enriched by the mellow yellow down and green and grey and white and black. The buttress ours and upon the conquered moans of ancient kin the ascent of freshness dealt with all the dangerous heightened maroons majestic in the summer sunlight. There stands bedrock weathered by hands in commotion, in adulation, in emotion, linking and sprinkling fairy dust into the crevices where henge spirals outward and inward. A moss of ghosts, the template sways neath growth in an occult timescale upon enchanted trust. When conferring the stone to a wish they descend as the sunlight castes upon the edifying green and stone circle played upon by the spirits which have regions that range time. The past unalterably determines our journeys in the present. The essence is that if life and co-incidence are harmonious then one follows a substitution principle so that life is time's fool and thought life's slave and we surrender to time; order in movement. However just as order is not such an advantage as a sense of chance can lead to different points of perspective, so time is only our name for the motion of consciousness. It is a convention. Overcoming the riddle of time is the transformation. Michael stayed until midnight.

## Chapt. 5 Atonement

It was so easy; procuring a job as a servant of the tower. The interview with Amaeigin was swift and once the protocol of references and wherefores was complete the old woman Michael was pressganged into keeping utmost secrecy about what Velouria said and did. He was told never to mention Ele'hail but to use Amaeigin's discretion. He stared up at the thousand steps spiralling above him and a butterfly danced into view. He climbed the thousand steps slowly and purposefully but anticipation got the better of him and he opened the creaking door. There was his love Velouria and the baby Ele'hail in her arms. He knelt down at her feet and spoke the words of his new form.

"I sigh, a hearty relief and dedicated sigh of pure, if I may be so bold, adulation about how tiny a form could give so much joy to one as wise wizened and worldly worn as I. That I may have a key which unhinges the spellbinding, hook-drafted-splendour contained within so cute a mind is awesome, magnificent. I have come to do your bidding Velouria" he said in all earnest.

"That which you can do for me I suppose" she replied "Can you free us from this wasteland, lift my spirits higher than the bleakness of this tower, answer my prayers at the eve of day and deliver my child from this imprisonment?" She asked, her eyes open and innocent in her demure desperation. "Facing fears of distance shaping teas that fall spiralling as the staircase down my reddened cheeks and the flag that flies so strong against the wind depicts the mighty conquest of welling love. So, I tilt my ear towards cupid's golden breast and dream of our salvation". Ele'hail stared up at Michael and for a moment studied the old woman's face in appraisal. She smiled and began to chatter to her mother. In a receptive manner.

"Some of these things I can, and some will be" Michael said. "Do not be disheartened for today the sun shines in from your window and the dayglow on your faces reveal a beauty strange but wondrous to my eyes. Many days have gone by with your child now a little person dependent upon you for all her worldly cares and so much more. You have done a fine job. An elegant woman you are and a hearty baby is this little one to whom you have lavished so much affection and wonder. She is all a beautiful daughter should be and none in this kingdom have such a carer as you will have in me. Do not be afraid. Do not fear but be the special person you are and your daughter will grow wise and strong to face each new morn with vigour and vitality. For even the bird on the wing is a prisoner of the sky. Try to do all you can to alleviate your incarceration and let the birds be your eyes and the wind your words so that all will come from those who rain on Amaeigin's parade. I have come to dedicate myself to your welfare and to help you raise this child so that she will see with the eyes of a hawk, feel with the summer breeze and sing with the skylarks which visit your tower. Though it is true you have been confined let not the spirit drop nor the mind wander from the place which is always your home. The free soul in which you have been blessed."

His eyes settled on the little one's face and she arched her back in a rolling smile. Her chatter forged anew as she saw the milk he had brought and he positioned himself on a chair opposite gently listening to the rhymes that Velouria sang as the baby guzzled and stopped then listening intently to every rise and fade in Velouria's voice began to drink again. Michael sat back occasionally joining in with a chorus of approval. The day was spent sometimes in deep conversation, always amazed by the little things in the child's play and recourse to nature that the tower concealed for it was a majestic view that the little child's eyes sparked upon from the sea to the east to the great town's rooftops to the west and the fields and forest to the north and south respectively. Always Ele'hail's attention was captured by the billowing smoke from the fires in the kitchen to the circling of the crows over the rookery and many a bird would spiral up to the tower until the eve of the day when the vast swarms of starlings descended from the corn fields of the north to the forests of the south. The sounds of the town would reach into the rooms from the business of the city and the fragrance of the dwellings permeated on the evening breeze.

It was while she was playing that Michael studied her, in-between helping Velouria. The breadth of her smile as a greeting, a reasoning, a creation was a glimpse of her happiness that Michael had lost. Wistfulness, a purpose was like the still boat upon the lake that washed over his joy everlasting. The kick of her feet as she beaned on the floor was fleet, beguiling, carefree a gesture of what she could and would employ from contentedness and the dexterity she would employ with her first steps. The skill of her clasp of her reaching for toys was the consenting relationship that dreams have with reality. Are they within reach like her toys to her grasp; contented, amused? Her thoughts were so calm so simple a sweet reasoning so desirable; so that what she could achieve would stay within her mind. She was learning in her own inquisitive way.

You are my joy and wonder
I have such faith in you
You are my tiny child
A child amongst none other
I love you till the seas run dry
And in you there can be none equal
Than the small child you are
And the small child you will be
I feel such a bond between us
An angel that flies above us
An angel which protects you
To be with you still
I wish you all the joy
I see in you
So frantically and empathically
The angel flies with you
You are in my heart forever
With you there can be no wrong
With you we will be strong
I love you till I depart
Yet never from my heart
I want you in all your babyness
I want you in all your days
To be with you is bliss
To see you and with you kiss
The brightness of the day.

Could Ele'hail be really so sweet? She could fulfil all that promise in her eyes. Monkeys made of gingerbread. Chasing her over all those hills for so long. Sugar horses painted red. Of course, the wonder was innate in the times spent with Ele'hail. Finding her beaning on her mattress in the morning completely content with her soft toys and blanket hugging softly her monkey while sucking her fingers. Those loving headbutts she made when she couldn't express herself. The chatting she gave to all situations. All those things to do, all those experiences to cram into the happy land.

It was a simple thing. A connection. Her dark eyes sharing a joke with you. Her comments upon her toys. Her tendency to do the unexpected, trapping love between moments. Transferring a sense of self from goodness. Ele'hail rendered his life complete and he hoped in return to make her day more fulfilling. He found himself wanting her crisp heartfelt and innocent ways. Like a bell sounding to prayer, she was constantly alert wonderfully feeling her way through, evidently happy with her enthusiasm. And to hold her, pick her up in one's arms and feel her nestle.

Velouria cared for her like none other. It was clear they had a special bond whereby Ele'hail would lose herself in mirth and jollity. Their moods and tentativeness understood each other like no other. As she descended her silly attentions on Ele'hail she was a one sensible and teaching, as frivolous and playing

A crumpled piece of toast lay on her lap. She munched on a piece of pear. Her giving mother pressed her with the wisdom of eating. She was not always keen. She investigated her world through touch like a ship expands knowledge of a map. She had reached the lake of attention and responded to her mother's cajoling. She loved attention and had recently got into the ritual of holding her hands up and smiling until you did the same. Armies up, armies down. She was very cute. Ele'hail was a joy. She looked like a little brown bear. She was soft and consuming. Her eyes pervaded the best times to him. Ele'hail lured and spurred one on to greatness by her simple virtue.

She hears the frog that croaked by the pond in the garden of the tower and she listened and smiled to a story the old woman told. There was once a green slimy common frog. Now this frog was hopping from the gutter to the verge and back again, playing chicken with stones because it was all he had to do. He could not jump at all trustingly on the road. He did not pay attention to the carriages passing for he had no sense, no green crossed tale to tell of. Hopping blindly and madly just like a real frog does leaping from pillar to post he looked very silly.

But what was that? Dab day die da dap- he could hear Mozart gently wafting from the other side of the road and as he leapt from the tears he knew, he jumped to the garden of a music teacher. His collapsed lung he had bourn from the gutter charged fruiting from his trunk to the ground and back again when he heard such a wonderful tune. He sought not ponds. The ponds that marvel and that gardens strike with red and white roses, but only the sound. In his crepuscular primitive brain, he thought that this music would give him the tail he had always wanted.

Frogs want tails because the fairy godmother of the pond says that they can have tails if only frogs marry. The legend of Mozart will grow my tail he thought and with patience, well as patient as a frog can be, he confided in the rock in the garden. His tongue caught a fly in one gulp. MM mm he thought. I have come across a stone in this Mayfair Garden and by honour it is beautiful. The music had cast its magic spell as the paper lantern gently swung.

With a leap and a croak, he leapt into the spell. The stone, a black and wily stone, whispered to him that life was kind. Was this silence a call from the hustle and burley road to what he had always wanted- a tail? He rested and opened his gullet to bellow "Croak, croak, croak!" After a while he beached his pride and so used to wandering aimlessly among the bulrushes he plucked up courage and asked the stone to marry him. This day is a day to remember he thought. "Croak" went his proposal.

Now you have heard of the princess who kissed a frog. The stone miraculously lit up in the moonlight a wonderful green. He swathed, he swayed, he swallowed and the rock passed into the frog. He had eaten the stone, which as if by magic turned as you may say into a frog. The frog croaked one last frog croak. "Croak!" The moral of this story is clear if you listen. Swallowing rocks has no tail at all to trace a thought to where it all began. One flat frog.

She could charm the bees from their hives. She was baby sound and vision, so soft; a cuddly babyness of softness and fun. She was all these things and she was Ele'hail. Ele'hail lured one into a dreamworld. She dreams of togetherness with her world. She realises the potential in every moment. She can be relentless and she redeems the past in you that has known the haziness of sin. She implores you to explore anew. She is content and captivated by the smallest of things. It is the detail she studies. It is the larger of concepts she dreams in puddles of reflection. Ele'hail wants for you to care then surprises in her response. She is a saucerful of secrets and a mignon de sources. She has will, tenacity and exuberance. She shows the point of trying. The point of sharing. The need of knowing.

The breadth of her smile a greeting reasoning; creative glimpses of her wistful purpose was the silhouette upon the lake that washes my joy everlasting. The kick of her fleet feet, beguiling beseeching a gesture of strong bearings of contentedness. The reaching is the concentrated solution to all that could be pressed from your tiny frame to us our homestead content. Your thoughts so calm so supple your cuteness so sweet and so subtle touring dreams so happy so achievable. I wonder wither they go or where they stay?

Hanging out amongst the pots and toys was his fatherly sense of duty. It was his duty to facilitate. Encourage. Help the woman of his dreams from her natural viciousness to a calm and laden existence. Her life was far from plain. She would paint and she would launch her keenness amongst the artwork like a crouching tiger. She was fiery and lithe and somewhat fun, slim and dapper and perfectly rounded, in fact in her garden with flowers surrounded she made an excellent love cat who'd prowl and preen and pounce all night for someone who takes you so romantically someone thus behaved as a slinky cat to walk with was a betimes a real turn on. Little aside about sex. Drives, ranting, requisite, addiction. There is a murmur aside the lake. A sensation. A lust. An appreciation of something spectacular. Arising hidden. Its ambivalence towards emotion. Its cadence of wonder. Its blackwalling of the sensitivity of a relationship. Maybe it'd be better without it. I could do without acting on it. I would do without its ignorance. When isolated it is nasty. Dirty. A mass of feeling gratuitousness. A kiss is not always tender. A caress is enough without it. A rational mind. A garden springing without it. One should not need its absorbing, self-indulgent addictive presence. When you look on it to condemn it is all consuming. It is an emotion I could do without.

Her face was one of familiar yet sumptuous good looks. Fixating upon her details each feature was fascinating in itself and as a whole looked so aware. She was so incredibly natural that she looked like an angel for his words of caring to assuage. She was quite vulnerable but strong and determined with it. He tried to be wholesome, respectful, considered. There were aspects he would not allude to. Ele'hail could be overjoyed with her company. She was a nurturing protective mother. Velouria and Ele'hail and Michael shared a fascinating warm relationship. They shared many a giggly session. Many a heartfelt moment. There would be attractiveness to the senses she stimulated between them and Ele'hail's recognition of this sense of fun. The times were extra special on her first birthday

> We share a thing or two you know
> Like birthdays and a tree
> We see each day anew
> And hear glad tidings be;
> Like the darling buds of may
> That the summer knows

# THE CHRYSALIS TIME

As the sound we want to say
As we wiggle up our toes

We stand about the magic bow
And blow arrows across the universe
To kiss the wind in verse
Feeling in watching a tree sway
Hang onto mummy's hand
For her song to lay
Like the bough of an oak a wish
That we could show our tutties
To the spoon and the dish

Forever I would if I could
Hold your hand and run into
The fields the trees the wood
Where the angry pixie lives just past
And the tin pot man clatters
And moon face sits and chatters
But pass them and you will see
At the top of the faraway tree
Is the land of birthdays at last!

The moon circled an apogee of faith for us to
share with the stars show of lost reminders. A tattered
and scared novel opens up in front of our dreams
leaching into the sky with wonder. The fairies chase
reasoning. Faith in what I don't see, hope in what I do.
Prowess in our hearts. I think I hear from your lips a
contented noise, I listen, your body framed to bring a
tale for us to season, thus telling grace upon your face, I
hardly answer reason but your face so gently climbs for
us to see this vision. I hardly know what stems the flow

of love between earth and sky yet look upon your smiling face and know it spans the mirth that considered opinion is reason for grace to be aware. So gently cling the hands so soft, so delicate in beauty there bathes and stretches for us to see and in our eyes portray a kindlier thought to justice; a connection that from your hand doth flow and still by morning you endure a happiness for us to know.

Yet still Michael wished for more than just a connection. His love lay neath the layered snow where fields of poppies once grew, beneath great blankets fit to sleep where oceans crash and children reap. His love lay valiant as a ghost the beam of dusty sunlight moist to tingle and spindle handfuls of dust onto the oil painted canvas rust. His love lay cloudy above the sleep so drowsily buried and spun under settling ocean deep where he was sound to have his sleep. His love lay admonished, like drying paint sticky to touch and thick and quaint just as my heart spies at last someone to spin my web of chance. And Velouria and Ele'hail were his art.

A stirring. Shooting ribbons from my mind I remit, respond to awareness, stitch by stitch, for we are links to the egocentric intention. Keenness exceeds the mast and the burden hearted stir from a rippling rending brow stretching many a question. Salt sprinkled and rage lusting the rocking subdues under us searching from the breeze blown time correction game. I falter I feel so clean. I feel so real. A stirring casts words from your mouth, your sweet soul to bind. So much wanting, no more forsaking. Shaken from gravities fold I throw my heart to time and haul it in. It sends the salty bar laden moments and romantic other worlds to find the strength. I find a walnut and recourse to motion. I stoop and pick a withered flower and times spring brings it back to life. The lines written merge and a task of influence caresses your throat. I resound that tried-and-true solution to the heat of the moment. I love you and your shoulder blades pinch in a daring movement of absolute softness. A rendition is heard. The world longs for you and by its milky white light I seal the whims which have troubled our waking night.

## PART 2 THE CHRYSALIS

### Chapt. 6 The Burning is Quenched

It was nearing Christmas and although to Amaeigin this was an abomination the festivities for the festival of darkness had been underway for some time, with trees of lights and sumptuous feasts planned. Michael fanned the fires of Amaeigin's wrath by telling Ele'hail of the nativity and that as a child she was special in this season. Amaeigin had stolen away the virtues of Christmas and had replaced it by a festival which exonerated the misdeeds of people in Miserablenow. Children were taught that they need not be good, just brave and willing. It was his deeds as a magician which kept the people subservient and all looked towards this season as an excuse to claw back riches and exploit others. A community which had been so ravaged by the time of wastefulness or so the Christian period of history was called ran rampage on the night of Yule.

Such was his intent to live with Velouria as was his dream he did not think of the repercussions of what was to happen that Yule. The morning began with the jeers and whistles of the eve revellers making their way home after nights of debauched drunkenness in the town far below them. Velouria lifted her head from the pillow and saw the old woman's eyes follow the curve of her nose and in study of her face Michael quite forgot how she stared at him, the old woman, as she got up to rise and take a bath. The town reminded them both of how they had never really clung to the same principles of management and persistence of style and wealth that preoccupied the town. They both felt a connection.

"You remind me of someone". She spoke. "Someone well in your speech the way you frame your words guard your inner feelings which are so bright. In the things you say and the response to my nature. You remind me of the baby's father. It is a funny thing but I almost feel he is there in what you say and do. I suppose it is just the way you care. We are very grateful you know of you being here I mean but sometimes I want him to be you. Here with us."

"It has been many moons since he was with you. You know great things happen through longing." Michael sat with his arm on her shoulder from her hair to her back he caressed her and as he did so he took a phial of liquid from around his wizened neck. His hand brushed her temples and he drank from the phial. There was a smoking hazy mist in the centre of the room and Michael was transformed back into the young man she had knew and loved. His white hair turned to a jet black. Her podgy arms into muscle. His drab clothes into velvet. Her beaked nose and sagging eyes into the dynamism of youth. He was where the servant belonged but now in her arms.

They sank into bed with Ele'hail between them and everything felt as it should. They smiled and studied each other's features as once they used to. They rose and walked round the garden no longer Michael in a stooping manner but upright and dignified they talked of their wants and hopes until the meal that was prepared yesterday was laid upon the table and they chatted knowingly of all the things they could do in their hideaway in the clouds. The night closed in and though Ele'hail was wary of this stranger to her world, she soon warmed to him and their fantasy was complete when it came to lying in the same bed. It was strange for Velouria and the fires in their hearts were this way quenched. After touching they felt as though the moons were racing in their heads and soon fell asleep. It was an impassioned and lengthy spell they caste and it lasted till late the next morning.

In the early hours Amaeigin had visited the tower drunk and scowling. He had stared into the light of the dawn until he realised that there were two shapes in the bed. His anger realised he flew into a subdued rage and had gone down the stairs vowing revenge. It was not long before it took shape. Shadows passed on the rigging-lined walls and an exodus was in motion. A procession of carriages left the gates and covered wagons followed.

Then the fires erupted in the town below. Small flickers were first seen, small patterns of red and yellow aglow until the larger proportion of the straw roofs were burning. Lost for words, lost through consequence, Velouria sat and watched, a paragon, a paradigm, the paranormal happening continued and a stirring within the mind encouraged her, endangered her, and gave face to her courage, her dependability while the fires engulfed this mortal coil. The cadence of candescence was like a small light growing in the angel's wings held aloft. A russet sunset in the town below, an assurance too fleet to fall came from Michael's lips, too sweet to see a rift in the smile in the world of themselves in the worlds of the tower dependable. Like a spinning jenny furrowing the fields of youth Ele'hail sat and watched. Her hands clapped and bubbles burst so that like a tree canopy surround the fires spread but did not extinguish the three of the towers.

A few stragglers left the town via the snaking road as the flames leapt, seeped and flickered through the speckled roofs. In his mind it was as though the seeping fans of fire were scales of a writhing snake, and that it was this serpent which swallowed up the town with fury. The snake rose. The snake billowed from the roofs and like alcohol fumes permeated the roof garden of the tower. It was like Michael was drunk on the fire. He wheeled around the rooms taking breathless peeks through the windows at the ensuing display of fury in the town below. The snake had entered the tower as madness? But it was not so. Small fires were erupting in the tower and Michael was busy extinguishing them with his feet, burning embers of the snake tongue from below.

The smoke was over the sea and the tower was the only visible part of the town above it. The tower was built with a dome at the top so that the chambers were protected from the ferocity of the fire's fury by a stone parapet. Michael shut the three in the innermost chamber and blocked all crevices from the smoke. They heard the snake spit and crackle. Smoke billowed out of gaps in the tower's girth and ascended upwards to cast a snake writhing in the garden. It covered the trees and the shrubs but just as it appeared a fierce wind blew and the small fire droplets which spat from the snake's mouth were pushed out to sea. The shroud of cascading fires blew out to sea and the fury below, like some mad cacophony of witches' fury in some dastardly plot failed to take hold of the garden.

Amaeigin looked back from the road and brooded over the smoke filled peninsular. With their burning bodies he thought lay the end of the past and the future. My granddaughter is no longer. She is but a puff of smoke which engulfs the tower. As he spurred his horse he wouldn't look back. His wards were to be annihilated for in his waking dreams he had found that they would be his undoing, his nemesis to destroy his power base. In the form of fire, the wrong doers of the future were to be quenched. His tower was not to survive. This was a noble deed in his eyes and only what Velouria deserved for going against his word. All around there was a red light.

Yet Ele'hail is working her magic; even as we speak. Her innocence is the red light. Are we bothered to come together in this weather, bothered as a bird in flight, by the harmony in rest the madness in the cave, the actuality in the slave, the conscience in the sky, the supposition in the lie, the elegance in the acceptance of the right, the majesty of an angel's flight? I ripen and grow in the swell, going against a tide of etched memory of twilight feathers. Between dear and tear is world of triumph, rested like leaves at her gate. What do we see in the night's ingenious shell- a natural little Babygirl from nature's promise and nurture's fondness? An interdependency, a connection; a red light, painted like the impression of a jumper so soft flown like the wings of your heart I beseech, falling like the resin of an autumn leaf fractals on the spectrum. Perceiving filled with belonging; reasoning forgotten like the afterthought of an airplane aloft playing like the magnificent musical mystery you teach silent like the crimson pinprick of snow I bequeath, bursting like the

ginger my taste binding. Red like a fire burning. For red
is the light that time flies the weave that is in your blush
Goodnight the apple of my eye
The welling of soul I have
Will never run dry
The tears of your dark star
Reflected by
The Limitless nurture
Capitol Purpose
Perspective
Dreams
All you had to give
And asked nothing in return.
Like a fire burning

Brave like the tide we have swam abroad, growing like
the seed of ages prepared experienced like the words I
have earned, founded on the blood comforting was
Ele'hail. Filled with ardour, spontaneity and reasoning
expectant like the river we are yet to ford, shining like
passing of time spent; yearning, wasted like the swig of
my blazing -brief like our lush crushed meeting. For red
is the light that flows the wave that is your candour, the
waves of time to envelope.

"My thoughts to you fly, borne out of concern- I
mean how else would you know that I had entrusted
you to the red light? The scene will hopefully be
onwards and upwards because each night I soar to
where you sleep. How else would I keep our angel in
check for these years?" As Amaeigin and Michael
thought these words their minds melded for a moment
then were lost to distance. The town's remnants were
still sporadically smoking and as day drew in the last of

the blackened and charred remains fell and scattered like dust. Similarly, the burning smells were replaced by the fresher winds of the tide. The three were to survey this view for many years to come perched in their chrysalis in the clouds.

## Chapt. 7 The Code of the Cocoon

The Three sat surveying the scene of the moon on the rise. Rain rumbled among the trees and saw as pan once saw- the celebration of a triumvirate and fortune in the raw. Michael spoke;

"This midwinter, like a crow among the trees, tarries among the bark and moves on the leas of poets to where you stooped in a river plenty. Has that river tossed our restless waking brood to where the patterns of river lost? The moon a weary and wondrous really the smouldering of latter days I have picked the last rose which flows along that river sinking clarity to the riverbed- on our crimson lips it did kiss a heaven-sent time under the rising moon- a vision of love"

Velouria, lost in bemusement, replied;

"I look at the weave of the loom and all thoughts inside your head and all things plentiful at night until I spied the bloom on this midwinter gloom the enlightenment upon which we tred is the sweetness of a riverbed and the rose a measure of how I care- for whom amongst the sky do I love but you as we find ourselves in a cocoon?" Velouria concluded. Michael felt insecure about the future of his lowly background and he told her so. She replied

"It doesn't interest me what you do for a living- I want to know what you dream of. It doesn't interest me how resolute you are- I want to know if you will risk looking like a fool for love, for your dreams and because of the adventure of being alive shout Yes! At the wildness of the moon" They tried to source their love from the moon on the rise and sustained themselves with God's presence, through all the empty moments before they were together. Their isolated togetherness in the chrysalis of the tower had two main effects

The first was a greenhouse effect. The simple life was unconnected to the rest of society so that the relationship was singularly intense. This brought dividends with Ele'hail's development as it was a hothouse of ideas and parental presence. Velouria became the spiritual and artistic guide to the world in the tower. Michael was part of this small eye, in the form of formal and scientific development. She hence had accelerated contact and awareness from the tower's enclosed space. Their reliance with no-one else to guide them made exploration of their ideas more intense in many a rare and intriguing way. Through their nurturing the three blossomed and glowed despite, or because of this, into a votary of practical ideas, softened to reflect the quarry left alive in them and bless their destiny for with a small eye to the future we saw the replenishment to absolve the scarcity a grassland of secrets under the blanket of clouds in the Martello tower. They grew vegetables and fruit in the soils of the garden and were self-sustaining with the chickens which roamed the yard. Hence, they had eggs and meat and seasonal vegetables. They had milk from the goats and learned to make cheese.

The people who pass you by in the land of the living are but a dream in the world of the tower, the eyes antipathy sealed are refracted by familiarity and good cheer does not depend upon strangers but rather making purple patterns in the grass leaves behind a certain mask of happiness, contentment often with the present- milled floss on the fields of a cycle of familiarity as a small child warrants completion. For all that glistens sparkled like snail trails or dew neath a possibility of years merging with your reality and an apogee of faith returned the love of truth's patterns seen. Prophetic, proactive Velouria conducted and played the keyboard in the room of the tower. So simple, black and white, swarthy notes countered by delicate tones doe ray me Michael screwed his eyes up in adulation of the play, of the sway of the hand which moved the subtleties between unerring chords neath hands of elegance moving grooving, seriously good; amazingly, enormously smooth. He gave; she gave. They took no wonder to play a tune of such thunder stole their minds. They lifted Ele'hail up as wings. Drawn towards the music he would drift while intensity moved across the yard when sweet inspiration took her. Much like the mist engulfing the tower in a spring haze. Michael spoke:

"Velouria stands for something special. Whenever I see you my senses tingle. I sense a delight in your arms so light and a caress from you is like a land full of glowing moon, forever an arrow from my heart soars to your crystal fountain, your immaculate mores. I love your deep eyes and fairy dotted skies, your temperament sublime, your words to my thoughts climb and all I am left is a heart that is deft to render to you these words and hope you remember I love you of course." Their love affair grew as Velouria replied:

"Bright and glowing the moon unfolds, is but the joining of souls into the eyes of one such as you reflected by our goals. Be happy and glad as we approach the springtime of hope and renewal, spreading and shedding features which vie for a place among the heavenly host. An angel borne by angel lines and always upon us shines this moment glad upon you to show all the passion and hearty finds for we are under this fitting moon to inspire and regulate light so far and we become like wings to Ele'hail."

The eternal meteor flew throughout the nights just to meet the sun again peeling back the night as time flew past. It was an imposition to be in the tower but it was no means a punishment. They were consumed in the jollity and responsibility of the little girl Ele'hail. The tower was enough. It was quite large and spacious. There was an inner chamber surrounded by five rooms in a hexagon with a spiral staircase leading to the little girl's room in the roof and a courtyard and garden beyond. There were three spiral trees, a small fruit tree area and a water feature in the middle where rainwater collected.

Velouria would dream of a softer understanding of things which guided her. She was not in a way which could be seen as better days. The experience of childbirth had given her insight into her own memories render from her like the hidden strength which kept her from negativity. Still negative memories and association sought her out. She was still perceptive and could change the inflection to hurt herself inside and doubt the everydayness which kept the family together as she took time to watch a solitary bird in the sky the code of the cocoon was how Michael had explained her to her. She was quite capable of experiencing all the effects of being together that brought happiness.

She was to be wrapped up in her cocoon until she was ready to emerge. She had been through trauma by being locked away from society and had forgotten about the damage in a pupal stage, putting a block on the scary thoughts and experiences and it was now time to work out the code of the cocoon by seeing what was not there for so long. To confront and to have faith. Give it to God. To not put herself through the pain of what had happened to her. For him to take away the responsibility. She had been growing slowly in her chrysalis. The delicate whiles the purloined lines of one bird against the skyline of her chastened bed flow stretch to occasion and grow and lie beneath haze green beige, the colours of chameleon. Dusted trusted loins splinter a recoiled sinister growl. So, each delicate line is misted like wood. And a butterfly descending from its song.

The things that made Velouria so special were innate and she created freshness in situations played out many times before. The evocative nature of her problems and her solutions thereof was a foundation for truthful conversations. People will draw on different ways to cope and some people deny who they are to eradicate the past and block them with multiple personalities yet Velouria was just a cagey eccentric, prone to manic energy. She learned to forego her intenseness and through Jesus, anger knew her name but she avoided the usual bitterness which is its willing accomplice, emerging from the chrysalis sanguine, affected yet free from its stifling influence. The love she aroused was brutally honest and she was learning how to delve and retrieve her memories randomly. She had coping mechanisms which absolved her and rid herself of the fear she had once inhabited. She once spoke of seeing herself as a small child in the tower and able now to prove herself free she had reassured her younger self. She found resolve and could dwell on the positivism which had always been innate but covered up in her. She was to all evidence an angel of the rain

The Lord is the stronghold of my life. The triumvirate formed hope in the release of and the worship of Jesus. They dedicated one room to prayer and meditation. Velouria had secreted away a bible and many of her songbooks were hymns that she had stolen from the pyre on which Amaeigin had burnt all the religious texts he could find. Something in the means by which she had suffered and turned her responsibility over to God had rested a balance in Velouria's mind. She had overcome her anxiousness by prayer and petition with thanksgiving. The family found lightness when requesting through praise to develop their senses in their isolation from society. But what of Amaeigin's philosophers' stone? They were glad and more secure. They felt more fulfilled as answers came in spiritual uplifting after requests were granted. Survival was not easy and Velouria would be wary of their success until the comfort attained by asking God's help to inspire and protect them. They found God where he always was; in their hearts and the power of the scenery which surrounded them. But whose was the room of light?

They were consoled by their faith and tried to follow the path of least resistance to seeing love and awareness of the trinity and soulscape they inhabit. The stone made it more real They were perhaps putting on armour against threats which increased their worries and discouraged their renewal. Faith in prayer made them sure of what they hoped for and certain of what they could not see. There was trust between them which was certain. Bonds which could not be assuaged nor delivered up to others. This was their personality in Christ. Their faith gave them a communion with the spirits. A pressure valve for their relationship. A certainty of values.

Just as the tower was built of strong foundations so Velouria wanted their relationship with God to be also. Jesus was the vessel for this. The fervent nature of their isolation within religion meant that there was an evangelical connection between the outside world and themselves. Michael was consolidated by self-awareness and observance and the faith he found was a guide and comfort. The gulf between them and the outside world lessened in the inner world they established.

Christianity's influence had been spread by missionaries from the continent until Amaeigin's power base had outlawed it. The vestiges of the good works still survived in the towns but Amaeigin had replaced it through a rural cult which thrived during his reign. Thus, dispossessed of their religion priests were seen as vagrants and treated without tolerance who had no place at court or in power. Those who worshipped a higher deity and code of the black star; belief, were threatened imprisoned and tortured.

While clearing away the vestiges of Amaeigin's influence the family were drawn to the philosophers' stone, a crystal prism which refracted light. It was of significance to Michael. With the cross of light in the centre, a fissure in the rock, it symbolised the receiving of communion and the freeing of sin from the world. It freed the mind to choose for in remembered stories it was used for three purposes, truth, beauty and good. It was a union of these perceptions and through the five senses they could be valued, protected and encouraged.

The Bible when placed on the alter opposite the philosophers' stone was illuminated by the sunlight. In the Bible glowed a single word; BELIEVE. *When the sunbeam burst through into the dusty room of light how a whirling column of dust seemed to whirl around. But this was not insignificant common dust for rainbow colours were dim when compared to the brightness that shone from the page on which it had fallen. The healing word BELIEVE from every grain of truth had the brightness of the beautiful and the good, brighter than the pillars of flame that led Moses from exile. From the word BELIEVE arose the bridge of hope reaching even the immeasurable love in the realms of the infinite* Hans C. Anderson. The tower was not so much a tower of Babel but Jacobs Ladder: Behold a ladder set up on the earth and the head of it reached heaven and behold the angels ascending and descending on it. The tower of the truth, beauty and the good was as it seemed to them- of whom should I be afraid?

## Chapt. 8 The Mnemic Eye

The second effect of the chrysalis was related to the first and was Ele'hail's method of escape. It was the effect of the mneme. The redeeming of memory reflexes to escape the dreamworld of her view from the tower emerging from the boundaries of the walls with the sky. She perceived the world as one of fantasy. *The hungry baby screams or kicks helplessly. But the situation remains unaltered for the excitation arising from an internal need is not due to a force producing a momentary impact but to one which is in a continuous operation. A change can only come about if in some way or other (in the case of the baby through outside help) an expression of satisfaction can be achieved which puts an end to the internal stimulus. An essential component of this experience of satisfaction is a particular perception (that of nourishment in our example) the mnemic image of which remains associated thenceforward with the memory trace of the excitation produced by the need. As a result of the link that has thus been established next time this need arises a primitive psychical impulse will at once emerge which will seek to re-cathect the mnemic image of the perception and to re-invoke the perception itself, that is to say, to re-establish the situation of the original satisfaction. An impulse of this kind is what we call a wish; the reappearance of the perception is the fulfilment of the mind. The direct path therefore is complete catharsis of the need i.e. hallucination is actually traversed* Sigmund Freud. She had a need to escape therefore produced a fantasy world to enact this impulse.

She bore the lightness gently and her interest grew gently for under the winking fluttering butterfly days was a feeling that soon the bountiful ideas would be hers just as the growing pains in a wink of wings was the lasting of achievement when occasions turned into the stem of emotion between the three to close upon the eyes of encouragement which blew a kiss asunder. The fantasy webs we design link purpose with the malign madrigal of our hearts. Yet to fly with the glorious possibility was just the acceptance of a universal principle of substitution brought to life by her favourite bedtime book *The Mnemic Eye*, whose pages started with the words: *The butterfly counts not months but moments and has time enough...* So, to subliminally climb up high into the clouds of softness of mink and abandon the jostle to think of a commanding vision of flight spreading virtue and honour above memory clamour was peaceful, wonderful -a world above. The skies the limit but what of heaven whose plan guilds our waking lives to reason, to guide us through caterpillar pupa and to convene upon conclusion with patience its relation? Where flight is the nerve-tingling meaningful so the treatment of life's mundane and fractious world is forgotten in our repose to the purpose of our existence. The spark of constant memory is a demand for the truth and mystery, the opposite to sods law –a universal constant of the substitution principle of the universe- contained within God's words. Her halo of honesty flies in the face of uncertainty. She would buy harmony, peace and resolution for there is to be no more pain. The spirit of creativity, fantasy and inspiration of the living proof danced in the trees without cautioning us to be careful, realistic, or to remember the limitations of being human. Yet it was, without wings, merely resting on one's laurels.

But to Ele'hail it was preparation for the day when her wings would unfold and hand the apparatus of the butterflies over to her. Ele'hail only knew of this place. He wondered how she dreamed. In fact, she dreamed of flying as birds do. Of transcending the walls of the tower to the places she saw from afar. The timeless sea. The forest banks and ditches. The sun-drenched corn fields to the west. She saw shadows of birds and butterflies and indeed these were her only visitors to her playground in the sky. She spent hours sitting on the grass fuelling her dreams with the arc and wafting of these insects in flight. From her spyhole in the sky endearing visions would pervade secrets in her sleep. Far–fetched yet in her dreams she could be anything she wanted to be. It was mind over matter. Ele'hail waits at splash point with an apple basket in one arm, three butterflies on another. Ele'hail let her secrets go to the butterfly lest the sky declared it as frothed and created as a cloud, laying down her requests to the heavenly host. The butterfly shines and shimmies with every breeze until they are soaking up the sun, sleeping. Flying above the chimney stacks. Her wings unfurled aglow. She would dream of flying with her parents and of angels in the sky beyond. She would believe in ghosts flying, so tough to be away from, above the positivism in a dove's crying, among spiralled fairy-bedded engrained beauty of butterflies, linking hands at sunset. To relax by fireside wooden seat while clicking crowing butterfly-black eyes of deer compete with owls at darkness to peer and peek at glances askance of our love of cheery hellos and enlightenment for salty pride to bring me down that follows an olive-green river to its source in yesterday's unknown. To see a laced, chaste angel revered in your hair, your daring care full of river and sky hill and high, moonfaced of midnight. That turns my sleep to save me in forgiveness sweetly.

Fixed with an eye to the horizon, fixed wing on airflow, fixed upon the icicle works like a talon in the undergrowth, anticipate fear and relax our minds with a pitcher of soul overflow and rejoice like a butterfly on the wing sweeping from roof to vale above in the sky we twist and turn, alarum and shimmy up to the heights of twist the point of turn above the singe and cackle we shed the ground like so many caterpillars pupating our prosaic wings above the light of reason, above the true truant of memories. Life is a hope that would be a rhapsody of grace where reality is lighter than the solutions in my mind. She drew power from these emotions across the skywaves and interpreted flight as a choice she would once make. The mystery demanded the truth of a universal substitution constant to burn the unicorn's evil through just as in her favourite bedtime book *The Mnemic Eye*.

Ele'hail picked this fantasy book which showed the way through faith, through fairy wings and butterfly kisses, to actually grow wings. Through a universal substitution principle. She wanted to be like the birds. She wanted wings of her own. To escape her prison. Freedom is a sentient being closer to further to closer, maturing slowly from faith to an angel. Leave like the tide, promising renewal, leaning close to the spread ripples of time's delight. What we will face will be the rocky outcrops of life's desires, patrolling pools of rejoicing and pools of mutterings. Our own forever. Till the moon singed back it's inside they lay forever to be whitened by small children who want to face the swell of the waves for its caress is as the sun ship-sea driven flag which takes heed of the mighty deadly passions. Ahead of the fabulous impetuous breeze. A passage, a flight.

They read it to her most nights before she went to bed but neither realised the significance of its root in the truth. They both prided themselves in a practical solution of happiness that they were not to take it seriously at all. Happiness, Ele'hail knew is a butterfly which when pursued is always just beyond your grasp but which if you will sit down quietly may alight upon you. Who knows where a little child's dreams go. In fact, they went to the dream trees, the spiral trees in the garden. They grew there and turned into magic in the babble fountain, just as in the book. Of what did she dream? Of the wild winds and flapping her wings with the air. Of soaring above and beyond green grass and trees. All enduring from her place amongst the clouds. These things made life so special to the ringing of the babble fountain.

## Chapt. 9 The Floating Note

Michael spoke;

"I will be patient said the saint in the waiting room I will be the sugar in the tea I will be the cloud in the destiny I will be the spanner in the works I will be the cross in the tattoo I will be the taint in the blood for you: I will be there for you." The triumvirate were there for each other during the mundane difficult times. Velouria replied

"The labours rip in the flesh of the morning's wish that the bones have broken of my love to you." The three were there for each other during the pleasant sun kissed times. Crickets in the afternoon, flying cordlessly in the sun sparking a rubber stamp on my health like a fruiting space in my bowl. Michael's hands seemed to learn perspective; an art form in itself sometimes but Velouria's endeavours in the artistry stretched from music to art to soulful inclusion, whatever the weather:

"Swan white body" spoke Michael, "Is this your wondrous smile? - cartelise windows to our soul, reminds my fingers I optimise your loving arms. Solace drips into my heart like a pinhole. To ride a white pony into the waves and breathe in air inside my bracken-blown dancing tune. A conical smile for a digging stone of my heart's principle." Velouria replied-

"Red lips speak in truths that separate the stars and moons and kisses emanate in trust they burst with vigour burst with lust." Michael replied

"Are these your wondrous eyes? My speck of constant wood; my rest, our plank. A tantalising presumption. Insipid, ambient, immaculate. For your melody to saw through." She spoke

"Blue eyes look beyond. They see each smile they feel each gaze and through a haze of lasting love they tell of future happiness. Bright and twinkling the eyes unfold are but the joining of our souls into our senses reflected by our goals." He spoke

"And we shed what is left of our summer skin-feathers your elegant plume- a mother cloak of living flesh. No words could share. The boundaries of language quietly cursed. No longer to be where else you would be. That with your grace is bowing" She replied

"Love of mine, the possibility, feather touch, honey shining that you hear me coming with soft ears so soft to touch listen to the silent vows and pray upon each secret shared they hear my soul, my wrongs, my rights."

The thoughts of the grey tower proceeded to hold a spell over the three. Ele'hail grew as the months passed and the years passed as variations on a musical theme. The talent of compassion warms us in our ivory tower like dimensions which glow and pigment my every hour on this paper trail loneliness is inspirations darkness, music inspirations light and we shed what is left of our summer skin. Time which cannot touch us is till flowing past the basket in the reeds and our mischievous heartfelt demeanour.

The spirit in the tower still attracted visitors from the coast. Along the misty turrets, laced and paced with moss tributes of birds came from low sunken valleys and the ridges of tree-lined coastal waters and fancied that they were nearing Thor bright journey's end in a cloudy sky. There were three, encased in stone; silky, smooth and ribbon tied the shell empty floats in the mud in this memory. Summers spied a damsel with skin so soft and gathered like a ring of browbeaten clocks on the rugged, rugged rock perched up so high in celestial haven reflected by a spectacular surfing sea below. They whirl the hours away sucking surf and rising tide, the honey-moon glory your memory. Some speed like the gulls to climb a rhythm and rhyme calling with desire and comfort, raging like fury to the heat of happiness and concern. Striding around hand in hand pattern lifting wreaking gulls scatter asking searching memories' future like purple acrid stammer the dolls dull hair and all is life is wonder.

An early summer secret. As the wind blew ghostly, they woke up. Ele'hail was fetched from her slumbering in the room above. She murmured, her hands clasping monkey and the fabric of Velouria's nightdress. Pallid wanderings of the night subsided from Michael's mind. The bed was springy and soft and Ele'hail greeted the scene with a smile. Years came and went. The three would sit together and eat jam and yogurt, on the veranda. The breeze would lift their spirits and breakfast would herald the brightness of the sun casting spiral fans over the ocean. They would depart to the garden lying on the grass, playing ball or Ele'hail studying something or other. She had an eye for detail. She loved small, intricate delicate things-sometimes she would be wishing these things to be her wings, feathers filled with pearls and sequins. She would translate the details of a leaf to be part of her growing wings. They would play with her wooden toys while making up rhymes and Velouria would put them to music later. The melodies would then muster Ele'hail's crayon strokes on paper in the afternoon which Michael would interpret as birds or people or dragons.

She communicated with words after a while and would mimic bird calls. She adapted to her small size and was soon moving all-round the place from her first tentative steps to running around the garden to practising gymnastics on the lawn. She recognised far more of the conversations though and her excitement was infectious. She would translate her feelings through exaggerated movement and sounds. She knew definitely what she wanted and would answer questions with yes and no at first then with statements and conversation. She would clap and cheer when praise was due. She would cry if she felt discomfort. Love flowed between the triumvirate and they were assured of each other's needs. They grew very connected although she was not over affectionate, she would nestle and giggle and push her head close to him. Love flowed between and around the three like a glowing light. Aware of each other's needs Ele'hail was not a needy child. There would be times when she needed play or comfort or fun but she would go to sleep without a peep.

The letter of sand's waves is the figure of the mother flails and relentless calls breakwater dairy sifts its alluring lift along the sky with fisherman's pie, arms unfurled upon this rock, the auteur' risk a wind-ascending theme to collapse upon the shore neath the tower recognizing priorities by the light celestial haven with the birds. Prayers were often said before she went to bed: messages from the heart. Their prayers ebbed and flowed

"Dear Lord, I know you need me as I need you like the golden key will remain the same and unlock the secrets of my heart my passions to arouse with my love till time itself is taken up into the skies that appears as good intentions in my eyes and I endure till forever's stars shake the pain away. Amen"

"Victims of jealousy are put to battle and dreams are set free when fears are vanquished for the devil's interference is quenched by trust in the unforged star that still shines for if you look into my heart, you will see that I trust in you father God so that he who steals shall suffer for no human hand will ever do. God will bring deliverance. My mind trips to expressions shared because through these we will gather solace to confront our fears. If I were tickled by the rub of love then a quill of pure amber would be my pen to tell of celestial, uplifting, hallowed, inspired events but the wind it came up strong and praised the miracle of life in the baby girl compounded by our depth of passion. God nurture her and keep her; for she is the joy of our lives. Amen"

Faith is like time and as time progressed so did their spirituality. Faith like time is a healer, a soothing precept for recovery and a developing sense to maturity. We mature though faith and live outside time in our spirituality. A tree grows and like vegetation given the right conditions our materialist life grows also. What is harping on about wealth without happiness? As the nightingale sings over the din. If ever there were a tune, then in its abundant faith it takes over dreams in a calm of nonchalance just as a tune heralds moribund rest. Nature is progressive and nurturing though faith and can in leaps and bounds transform our lives and priorities out of time and our perceptions of natural growth. They were cocooned from the outside influences.

We are able to realise our potential in a spiritual dimension. Linking hands neath open skies with trust hidden as lanterns shine in the dark, they proceed with caution's whitening hark. Grace with voices clear and soft, the games of jollity of praise above of laughing glinting birth of Jesus at Christmastime. A cracking frosted lake of need, the icicle works of thrusting steed of ice and snow the frost covered birth exposes the gaiety of cold red noses. Neath wonton sky we peer and peak and grace lands on dreams of playing near animals and landscapes we see from afar to fly over this white dust this Christmas.

Ele'hail would sometimes speak of growing and Michael would tell her stories: Eddy the elephant's eyes were blue, blue as the azure sunsets of Africa. In his little stall he was praying to his hat. God knows I'm good, he thought. The width of his brimmed hat was his lonely life's measure. I'll sit here till I grow, he thought. His big floppy ears and his hairy chin bent down to drink his milk. My corner of the morning I love best, he thought. The straw was small and yellow. One daddy elephant promoting the day bellowed. The baby elephant trumpeted and frowned. He was as happy as he could be. The food and the day passed away until twilight. He cried. He had no fear though. Eddy could anticipate that. He liked polos, he liked refrigerators. He liked throwing in the towel with his trunk. But basically, he liked to eat the moon, in the reflection on the water. He spoke:

Is there anything more wonderful?
Than the illusionist's enthralment
Over the shoulder to hold her
Of milky white romance?
The answer is plain;
It is when I have
Tusks!

As he was sucking the water from the pail, he remembered the pale moon shafting fairy dust upon his ears, and touched the milky-white-likeness with his hairy chin and smiled a silly smile. The very way fathers do. He looked up at the tree, he scratched and swayed. His eye focused, the coned stream in the flash of moonbeams was back in the wake of his hat, the size of the moon. The lights went up

Bravo, the incredible baby elephant! The weird wind applauded and aah the senses. The balls he could not juggle could not protect him from the peeling of applause. But he felt no fear. The chimes of freedom from his ankle bells could not fell him. Dazzling tricks and amazing feats of skill were performed. The ridicule passed him by and a wardrobe loomed. He crept inside and the magpies hushed. The rabbit warrened wood concealed him and he dreamed of growing tusks.

## Chapt. 10 Nothing Ever Changes by Staying the same

The best of change, compromise, could be the singular most searched for paradigm for all problems. A balance in a carefully moulded existence. For Velouria it was of import to redeem memory reflexes: recollect not subdue, forget and forgive. To accept what had happened and put it behind her. Honestly to track the tears, but not to give in to the bleak situation. The situation was evolving to a mnemic certainty. The situation was already in balance. Yet as they spent evenings, they imagined the outpouring of wisdom that could follow from, what could best be described, as escape. The dusty books brought realisation of the skyward hopes that the three had been having from their vantage point in the sky. Each would look towards the sky as an escape from the prison of their minds and bodies. Velouria's was a prison which connected her past with the present. Michaels was an inability to connect the pleasant nature of their existence with hope for the future. Michael told Ele'hail stories to allow her to escape from the tower but they were only imagination: There was once a dandelion, which dreamt of being a real lion, a gruff and penny-copper in colour. To view the twisted wild green grass, she pulled herself into openness, like a gardener's foot and sliced off the stem on the step with a heave ho. There. There were a basket of mud, an old tire and a raspberry ripple ice cream. She went to the worm for help. He said "I will wibble wobble in the sun"

"That is no lion!" said the dandelion so she set off to the alley to talk to the dung beetles. They asked her what she had up her sleeves. "My arms" she said and huffed off to the conservatory where there was a money spider on a plant and tree's shadow.

She said the magic word and hey presto she was a fine African lioness. Daddy came in and said she shouldn't blow seeds in the house. "Growl!" she said. Mummy was playing piano. "Growl!" she said and then added, "What time is it?" and with that she was just a plain pretty girl again who had been a lioness.

They compromised for their ivory tower held a fascination. It had the attraction of their security. Velouria spoke of it one spring day-

"Nature by morning climbs in my heart by noon sustaining by evening we hark the day and as the moon lifts its veil, nurture's moment within us will last forever. Web of protection and fervour the moon absconds as the blue glass wave lifts her hand and strokes the golden shores for, we share excitement enticement normality here. We will last as undying souls in our paradise created by us cherished by us remembered by us. A beginning of undying love to share and blaze with passion." The tower was like a daffodil on the peninsula. Time's envy does wait awhile as the daffodil towers her head still stooping though drinking from crystal waters her very soul is rekindled and she trumpets a fanfare. From where this lonely tower now is, a host of portalled butterflies' dwell then take flight in a multitude of minutes her heart overwhelmed by their chrysalises.

Michael replied "This pilgrim maze is a world apart the heavens, which open too often in this season. The sea a lake of shell-like rhododendrons riding on the back of reason below of smoothness blushing when we stay, together through this vegetative swathe, there is security down this milky way. Meet me by the apple trees and we will wander awhile, take our rhythm from the wind and hark a melody from your incredible smile that the moon shafts down upon from above, the rain wages too rough that passion in isolation leads to love, so we moonlit walk to the well and throw pennies in as they drown the passage we read to spell the passions caused by the killing moon the breath frosting from above to the temperance of a dove- is their ever security in love! One does not have to blindly wish. It is just there, like faith."

It was Ele'hail's revelation really. Her book *The Mnemic Eye* was through her imitation, to be played out. It spoke of crystal-rainbow waters which joined wishes to reality between the three spiral trees in the babble fountain which flowed from and to the pools of rejoicing and mutterings. The waters instilled belief in a physical manifestation of these through a universal substitution principle of a chrysalis which would bring her wings. Little rainbow swirls and dreams are often just as it seems little rainbow prayers for little rainbow people caught between the bright and dark, a fairies wish a gremlins kiss, for all those who listen let it be heard Velouria and Ele'hail are little rainbow swirls and dreams are often as it seems little rainbow prayers. The book said.

This flow of energy between the three spiral trees flooded the memories of telemetries and wing flow from the birds into the wishing dreams she had been having, to transform her human form into that of an angel. An angel only wins if it sees a person turn from crest fallen to real, not fade away. Good and bad, right and wrong seems a lifetime away. Comfort and confidence told way back hence was to her mind an angel's shrine, lost in a balloon of hope and futures' taste on her lips the wine of another year. So, to the smile and tears of a little baby girl on her face linger like a woman's back in the wings of a lover that maybe we were born to be together mingling with circumstance. Imitation picks you up like an addict but it is hard not to want to be like them on your way to some everlasting. Be happy and glad as we approach the springtime of renewals toast where features vie for a place among the heavenly host. An angel borne by angel lines and always upon us shines this moment glad upon you shower all these passions a heart finds. For Ele'hail is the gentler rainbow to inspire and regulate light so far and in your ways a moment's twain embracing our celestial colours?

Moments are to make a link between our dreams and our purpose. The source of the morning is but an atom brewing on the horizon of encounters beguiling our memory but the triumvirate had none of these. They were cocooned and there was no way Michael would let outsiders fuck with their heads. Through their warped belief, through arrogant style, through capture. Through endeavour they would find a way to be content with their tower. Those people too content with their ignorance. Too scared. Too bad to believe. None more so than Amaeigin. Michael thought so much of Velouria and just pitied Amaeigin for his inadequacies - combination of his hope's vision, his screen of flowing opinion and the seriousness in Amaeigin's evil undertones was healing her. It was all that mattered. She had a way of bringing out the significance of life. It kept him, cherished him dazzled and sustained his senses. The three could fascinate their resolutions so who needed the outside world? Least of all Amaeigin's evil society. Their experience was absolute reality and their inclination to innocence flowed through Jesus.

Wishes like a tear were as happy as dances and as solemn as grace as their closeness unfurled. If taken in jest, life was as hollow as the laughter invests and if taken in solemnity then honesty also treads a lonely path. The key was a balance and a dawning of development facilitated by talking moments of resilience whereby each could change holistically and organically into the reminders of their roles which the brain renewed as hope just as the atom on the horizon renewed their dreams. When the concentric circle breaks the red into orange turns the feat into destiny burns and the inside moves outwards when the sun on a distant hillside shines the same reminder stays until hillside grass remains the tread of our dreams. When the sunlight expunges darkness; an inner sanctum reveals a haughty grace in conversation and seals our fate. Just as Amaeigin's words and actions had abandoned the three so their dedication to each other revealed the true essence of what it was to dream. And these dreams were captured by the spiral trees above the streams of missing moments.

They looked into the pool of mutterings. Captured innocence in a glance that we may share given half a chance. Beyond the waterline there seemed to be light from another world and if one cupped one's hands to block out the shadows a fuller dimension could be seen, a subterranean netherworld of flickering dancing, flying shapes emerging which had an expanding effect on your own reflection. It appeared as though you had wings.

Indeed, Ele'hail would sit close to the edge and wonder at the reflections of this world. For Ele'hail does not see as numbers, resolute and fixed, but wide-eyed as another new dimension beginning. For Ele'hail does not speak through words but the contours of the world she inhabits and captures the resonance of the water through her own transparent thread, like the contours of her face it captures only the heart which beauty everlasting is translated from ideas of innocence as her hand brushes the bluebell waters; a youth's open surprise.

Velouria sat on bedrock hands with Ele'hail in her arms emotion alighting fairy dust onto the water where spirals fill the watery depths.

"If they are only pretty beneath reflection's mask in the hallowed ground of footfall-wended-water, sketched etched pathways to fly into, graded, laced, chaste revered in your hair, your daring care full of river and sky, hill and high, moonfaced of midnight then save me in forgiveness sweetly to loll our child to sleep." Her open-ended trust would keep, as the shadows descended the edified green and bluebell haze played upon the spiralling images emerging from the pool of mutterings, her parallels alive. Velouria spoke:

"Mirror images to me smile of plenty and eyes that raise the spark that cries between the sighs and magic moments lain to rest. Parallels are like dreams that borrow whiles and many a halo in an expanse of happiness, a mirror image, her face to see. As we look into this pool's reflection" she faltered "-I see her with wings"

Michael was sceptical and told them both a cautionary tale:

### Wanteefly

Rolling over in the clover
The worm alighted upon
A wicked old chameleon
And asked him a question rare
About the way that nature dictates
Brought his question to bare
A travesty of beauty
Upon themselves in his moonlit lair.

How do I become
Like the butterfly I see
The one who sits upon the leaf of the tea
Those resplendent wings as a kite
Bountiful travellers of the air
Whose regalia so bright
A travesty of beauty
I behold from the light.

Said the wily chameleon
Jump upon my tongue
And I will send you up on wings so strong
You are wrong! And he munched the earth until
Out of his clutches
Was his will
A travesty of beauty
A mystery meal upon the bill.

He headed up into the grass
And spied a grasshopper
Rubbing his arse
How do I get the wings to stretch
Upon the winds and fetch
A travesty of beauty
Far from myself this wretch?

This is easy said the grasshopper
Jump into the web
For the spider will encase you and ebb
Your life away to change
And decide as he did lie
Preparations to fly
A travesty of beauty
Cocooned within the spider's eye.

Days went and weeks went
And the spider attached
Wing of bee and feeler of ant
One day appearing with glee
From silk and web
A butterfly emerged from head to knee
A travesty of beauty
A merge of ant and worm and bee.

Yet to that worm as he lay
Upon the tea leaf so gay
Was his life's reward
A morbid imitation of nature's hoard
A travesty of beauty
Far too far from delight's cord?

A fabrication of the three insects
He was
Neither one nor the others cause
He took on each one's ugly absurdity
He was a meaningless entity
A travesty of beauty
Parody of wanteefly in a word.


Ele'hail however was adamant and replied

"Our deepest fear is not that we are inadequate, our deepest fear is that we are powerful beyond measure, it is our light, not our darkness that most frightens us. We are meant to shine, as children do. We were born to make manifest the glory of God that is within us."

**PART 3 THE BUTTERFLY**

**Chapt. 11 Metamorphosis**

Eleh'ail sat down with Michael and Velouria on the island of the pool of mutterings and the water sang, the waves of time to envelope, sang of the story so far with a glistening upon the breeze. When the afterglow of the sound was fading the triumvirate set to opening the sluice gates and pouring blue and yellow dust into each opposite stream which circled the spiral trees. They had been very happy in their tower in the sky and eleven years had passed since the child Ele'hail was born. The pool turned a translucent green. Next Ele'hail set free her butterflies from a basket which she had reared from caterpillars and they settled upon the spiral trees' branches. All that was left was to pour in a little of the fairy dust which Michael held in the phial around his neck and say the words instructed in *The Mnemic Eye*.

"Are you ready?" said Michael. The noise from the trickling fairy dust explained that tomorrow would bring a new hope of compassion and, of wings. Ele'hail's dreams were to be captivated by *The Mnemic Eye's* words and, she hoped would be her escape from this tower. They peered at the widening circle of birds from their roosts and she began- "For wings that shape the love of the trust we hold, cautions a style of a mind that creates the intimacy of the trust we could motion to brighten our while of wings which make the fun of the trust we mould, notions which broaden our mile that initiates the truth of the trust we told to emotions which widen our wings to fly in the chrysalis time. Vermis quia resurrexit."

A strange dust flowed around the three and they were about to speak but were held mute and dumbstruck as the butterflies flapped above their heads in a frenzy of wings and spiralling dust which seemed to come from the very roots of the spiral trees and drift over the pool of mutterings. Their eyes drooped and soon all were fast asleep. Neath the evening breeze the paisley butterfly stood and arched her back against the last sun's rays. The sun peeked from the west down, like an arrow through the rain. Once in a realm of wooden ideals in light sheets she hid in the shadows of her wings under the spiral tree's melody. Feathers floated gently in the breeze and she danced to a tune of the rosehip ballet of the wood to her old friends still asleep.

The trees' defence was the butterfly's escape, gone in an instant to the crying thigh. So tired of everything the triumvirate slept as the butterfly flapped and the light slipped into the dark. But the moths the quickest flew. It felt as though the sheets of rain would last all night. The moths ran with the dark, saturated like unopened envelopes they hid with the dead as the drips fell outside and ran like rivers down the window. In the morning the butterfly pricked up her wings as she looked at the three asleep around the pool of mutterings and glancing from the rock, she found only her reflection. Still in the water.

The next couple of days saw a transformation of the sleeping triumvirate. A pallid coloured skin grew over and enclosing their bodies. A light brown colour stretched over them at first the webbing of fleece then the softness of silk wrapped around them so that their forms became merged and their features obscured. A veined web grew over this and the pulsating veins soon covered the skin until the outer exoskeleton became a crust of different layers hardening as the time crept on. The feeling of security and warmth was the result enclosed within their cocoon and their individuality was obscured as the brown leaf-like structure grew around them. They still breathed but their inhalations were shallow and soon moulded into a pulse of the veins on the chrysalis. They had become overwhelmed by the secret of *The Mnemic Eye.*

The chrysalis was a place for words and experiences of the triumphs of love and ages, glorious, and inside the renewal of compassion and outside the depiction of stasis wrapped in ages present. Inner ways and outer horizons. A mind map in the wrap of a heartbeat. The impression was that the three were engulfed in a dream and the world was comfort. Heat was exchanged with the outside according to Boyle's law which advanced its criteria with the longing and hopelessness of flight. Yet inside there were flights of fancy, sensations of care and joy and transference of feeling to replace regret with integrity, awkwardness with composure, influence with desire. Their bodily development was the impetus coursing through their veins to delve into different journeys to find the truth. Ele'hail visited Amaeigin from this cocoon state. She led his dreams like a stay jewel fruiting along the dairy path, daughter to the stars chasing the meteor's bloom until the coppiced lagoon red setted with explosives let her heart linger on behind glass, the starry daughter of pearl thrown and crumpled to kinship appeared to him as a vision of a moth as he was reclining in his stately chamber.

"To find that we are free to be chosen by the sound of our own voice" she spoke. "Freedom is a sentient being closer than further, further than closer, maturing slowly. I come like the stars, engaging renewal, leaving spreading ripples of time's delight. We are free to face life's rocky outcrops, patches of rejoicing and pools of demise. Until the moon singes back its inside I will remind you of your wrongdoings." As she disappeared into the dawn's light the man we lost for words shone elliptically from shoulder to shoulder in a winking and dramatic art of guilt and remorse in a meteor showered tyranny that he had succumbed to... He read aloud from a poetry book by his bed:

> *The caterpillar on the leaf*
> *Respects to thee the mother's grief*
> *Kill not the moth or butterfly*
> *For the last judgement is nigh.*
> ©William Blake

He let the moth fly from his balcony and off into the dawn. It instilled in him the decision to visit the tower and he gathered his best men and scaffolders around him in an entourage to set off for Walton and his old power base.

The slanted hills overshadowed the journey as if a gaoler watching his captive. They braved the plains where the wild men lived and traversed the wooded areas much quicker. They rounded a headland and entered the downs which, shrouded in mist, the tower suddenly loomed up at them without expectation. Memories seeped into the subconscious and Amaeigin felt his lifeblood thicken as they camped outside it. On inspection the stonework was found to be sound and that day the men were instructed to build scaffolding up to the top of its innards. It would be incredible had anyone survived- yet there was his vision. He cupped his hands to his mouth and then his ear and listened. There was a faint fluttering noise.

He pushed open the door of the old staircase and the stole moments of malice as a cacophony of butterflies fluttered and swung in the air past him and into the stone tower. Secrets to the butterflies never uttered a sound. The garden was a regular butterfly haven and his men could be heard discussing this omen. He silenced them and inspected the rooms and bed chamber. He found signs of life albeit musty and dampened by time, yet no-one was present in any of the rooms. He stretched himself in the garden's light but his eyes transfixed upon the island in the pool of mutterings. There was a decaying tree stump some six feet long on it. A brown casing of some sort which sent his fear level to burning point so he shunned it to turn away. No sign of anyone. He stared at the tree stump. A brackish smell was in the air and the thing looked almost translucent and veined in the sunlight. It was a decaying wood of some sort he thought and passed it by to look out from the tower's walls. He looked down. No-one could have escaped from this place from such a long way up he thought. But he found no charring nor burning of the place as he expected. It was a butterfly house, that was all.

His menacing continued and all stayed with his brooding as he muttered to himself "I can see a woman's face in this wood" he announced. Amaeigin looked confused but then dismissed the idea. "We are leaving" he instructed his advisors. "This place has bad memories. Seal up the door and knock down the scaffolding behind us."

Does the soul convey the answer to the riddle of time or does the riddle convey the soul? The past unalterably determines our journeys in the present. The essence is that if life and co-incidence are harmonious then one follows a synchronous universal substitution principle so that life is time's fool and thought life's slave and we surrender to time; order in movement. However just as order is not such an advantage as a sense of flight can lead to different points of perspective, so time is only our name for the motion of consciousness. It is a convention.

The spark of constant memory (i.e. perspective) is a demand for the truth and mystery. The opposite of sods law is a universal constant of the substitution principle of the universe contained within Jesus's words. His halo of honesty flies in the face of uncertainty. He would buy harmony, peace and resolution for there is to be no more pain. The spirit of creativity, fantasy and inspiration of the living proof danced in the trees without cautioning us to be careful, realistic, or to remember the limitations of being human and the sleeping Ele'hail awoke. As she did so the inner casing on the chrysalis began to expand and the visible sign of this was the cracking and splitting on the surface. She pushed her hands upwards and levered the split casing upwards and as she forced a gap between the crusts, a ray of sunlight fell upon her face. She was relaxed, purposeful and her identity sought resolution. She kicked her legs to wriggle through the ever-increasing gap at the top end and her body slithered upwards. She rested then plunged her arms out of the split. Her head saw the world outside and its familiarity calmed her.

Yet. Where were her parents? The realisation that she was alone transfixed her. Her parents were there by her side when they had fallen into stasis so many moons ago. Yet at her side now were wings. She had achieved the impossible! And her heart rose and fell with this thought. She prised her body out of the cocoon and sat panting in the sunlight. Her fragile form had been transformed but the departure of her parents? They lay within her still and they appeared as visions to her confused senses. Her mother was rising into the air yet as her father rose also, he faltered and began to be seduced by his previous form. Winds dragged him down and across her path.

Her wings were emerging, beating in a veined rhythm, yet one began to lose its life blood as Michael's image descended. His heart which had been given to the wing was faltering and the wing had stopped expanding. He had faltered in his life and his guilt and burdens of existence led were causing an icy wind to drag him towards oblivion. Just at that moment Velouria's soul hesitated from the light in the sky and Ele'hail repeated a word. BELIEVE. Calmly. From the word BELIEVE arose the bridge of hope reaching even the immeasurable love in the realms of the infinite. Michael's soul began to resist the icy wind and as he did so his trust of Amaeigin and their refusal to condemn him mercilessly, paid off. For Amaeigin arose from where he was observing Ele'hail.

His heart full of redemption he repeated the words from the book the mnemic eye and wilfully massaged the weaker wing. "For wings that shape the love of the trust we hold, cautions a style of a mind that creates the intimacy of the trust we could motion to brighten our while of wings which make the fun of the trust we mould, notions which broaden our mile that initiates the truth of the trust we told to emotions which widen our wings to fly in the chrysalis time. Vermis quia resurrexit."

The life blood coursing through it returned and the icy winds turned their attention from Michael who fought to retrieve his upward ascent towards Amaeigin. Moments are to make a link between our dreams and our purpose. The source of the morning is but an atom brewing on the horizon of encounters beguiling our memory. Yet heaven is real as Jesus promised- *In my father's house are many rooms; if it were not so I would have told you. I am going there to prepare a place for you* John 14.2. If we strive for its glory; it will reward our trying.

The winds instead turned focus on Amaeigin's dishevelled form. He rubbed both wings harder and as he did so Ele'hail revived but he started to feel the icy pull of his own demons on the icy wind. He had courted the ways of man and they now dragged him towards the world of men. He held Ele'hail in a steadfast gaze. "Forgive me Ele'hail. Here is my seal. Claim the kingdom. For you are my forfeit enchantment." And with that he died.

Ele'hail turned to the sky and as her wings beat the air low and strong, her parents disappeared into a pillar of light and her visions faded. Yet she heard one sound. That of Jesus saying: "Take strength, for you are the only one, cover your bushel with innocence for where your treasure is, your heart will be also." She arose and went to the parapet. "So, distance doesn't care, does it?" She enquired to the birds circling below as they had always done yet never. She spread her wings. A view for a new horizon pierced her soul. Skipping in the meadow a mist formed. A ray of light from the sun pierced the cloud and a hundred rainbows formed. With the new coloured light birds danced down onto the rainbows and became butterflies. The butterflies spiralled in a flash of pastel shades and flocked back to her. They kissed her skin and settled on her arms. Attaching themselves she raised herself upwards and engulfed her and she had wings. Upwards she went, transformed higher and higher into the sky, into the clouds then she fell as rain. She had gone beyond the confines of her tower. She soared through the haze.

## Chapt. 12 Emergence

Freedom says as she laces the knots in the journey- where does it take us? and with what progress the pilgrims should have to relinquish the sights of loose attractive tops to retrieve their progress to the summit of lost cloth. It was Easter but the gosling minute will yearn for inside in dreams of renewal. Well-practised in the art of sweet turn twisting frugality, before, through the mists of Miserablenow the Walton tower stood impregnable. The lamb to the slaughter they were minted at the foundry of the universal substitution principle, deriving liberty's bell from virtue. Levelling pangs to the red sky, the bells of heaven had only a positivity to it all.

Ele'hail flew, transfixed for a moment on the low ground before her;

When the gleaming, sparkle breaks
The beauty of intimacy
I soar above my fragility quakes
Swift flood my blood in coursing flow
The veins that should my wings aglow
Rise assuredly above all and mighty
Fly straight and level in solid state
I rise above from this parapet
No weight to bedevil this swanlike gait
Rise assuredly above hill and turret
Crack fire and brimstone in the night
Lest trumpets tone begets the flight
Rise assuredly above vale and valley
Off into the blue horizon's sky
And yet I wonder why

The coloured lair beyond we go
For honesty's answer rang clear of hue
The coloured sky I see my view
I veer towards in air so lofty sings
My wonder gone between my wings
My precious hopes my glorious nature
Of a girl returned a winged creature
The eyes see as a realisation
True vision of closeness
From this vantage point in the sky.

She skipped over the river beds and swooped over the fields. She danced in a field; it was pretty there. Here were no people, no men or women. She felt safe. She touched her wings mid-flight and smelt the daffodils growing alongside the lush grasses and poppies. She landed next to a village and watched the early morning business consume the night's pallid veil of sleep. At the break of dawn, she swooped up to her tower to land by the pool of mutterings. She remembered her father and mother kindly and looked into the hulk of soft tissue. They were not there, as she presumed. The presumptive breeze shook her from her stance and she left a flower on the chrysalis. Was this what she had wanted? Most revered. It seemed somewhat cruel and hard, as frightening a departure from the comfort of her previous life as adolescence had ever been. Still, she swept up her wings and lifted from the ground. She would seek. She thought. She would find. She thought.

Yet first she would bury Amaeigin. She had not known his callousness. Only the pathetic form which had shown her kindness. He was easily lifted into the cart and she dug a hole in the hollow of her fruit garden. She planted a sapling over him and prayed. She toyed with the seal ring in her hand like a magpie. She decided upon dinner. She would have eggs for breakfast and sacrifice a chicken. Did she now rule the roost? But she was no bird. One just had to look at the chickens. Out of a door a honey coloured-coated cockerel strutted. The hens looked up and as they laid their eggs they clucked. The blood dripped onto the straw. None of the hens knew how to fly, like the trolls under the bridge they were trapped by their ignorance. One cluck meant brilliant, two clucks meant wonderful, three and they had forgotten why they clucked in the first place. They were always happy at least as another egg slipped through the shoot. She would not be hungry today.

The chickens were waiting for when forever is through. They were talking, well clucking, the skies not hidden from them yet they would not fly away. They could not or they would not. They were dazed like the blueness of the sky, just a rumour in their burley world. "I still want you!" one clucked then paraded a goosy smile, a silly but curious smile- why did they stand around all day when in a twinkling of an eye they could be airborne? Well, the females were busy feathering then defeathering the nest and the male was looking to strut those last words before they were plucked for their feathers. They did nothing but wait, still it made them happy especially when it rained and they did lay lots of eggs.

The chickens were attempting to lure the cockerel into the pen. "A pound a dance!" they clucked excitedly. "Tough cockerels, rough cockerels, darlings are we all! Cluck" went the hens. "Cluck cluck" went the hens and laid a whole clutch of eggs that fell down the shoot "Come in!" clucked the chickens. "I still want you!" dreamed the dreamer. But she stopped at the door to pick up a feather

"Sometimes one has to make one's mind up" she said with the feather in her hand. For after her stasis she was enormously hungry. She looked at her form in the pools of mutterings. Her body shimmered and rippled in the clear water as she stooped to drink. She sensed something over her shoulder reminiscent of her father by her side still but it was only her wings. She flapped them and swung them to and forth. Then rocked herself in the sun. She turned and went to her room. Time to rest she thought.

She had choices to make- what would she do with the seal to the kingdom. Could she realistically wait while she learned from the birds' turning acrobatics and their skills until she was proficient? They zoomed and played with her as she practised that week and her childhood had prepared her for achieving excellence through her observations of their dynamics, drawn to the sky as she was. Now she was neither child nor human so she stood unaccepted in principle from what she was and what the humans in the kingdom expected of Amaeigin's seal. However, she was to have solace in the most unlikely of forms – in the guise of a worldly figure which had also the dwelling of the tower and whose dimension she was about to realise.

A shape kept appearing to her, heralded by flashes of white light, in the space where the chrysalis had been on the island of the pools of mutterings. She made out the form of an otherworldly figure in a long coat from her vantage point in the shadows. He noticed her there but seemed unconcerned. It was no ghost yet a man undoing and closing a portal in what appeared time and space to let light through from another dimension. *From the gate thrown open issued beaming, a beautiful and mighty Thing of light, radiant with its glory, like some banner streaming victorious from some worldly-overthrowing fight: my poor comparisons must needs be teeming with earthly likeness; for here the night of clay obscures our best conceptions of the portal passed.* ©Byron She decided she must pluck up courage to speak to him, if indeed it were a man from the shadows; she was to have him speak to her.

One dusk she decided upon an input. There she had said it. "Hello there!" There was certainly an input. But he looked so surprised that she had noticed him that he went into a verbiage of confused ideas. An age passed between the first sentence and the next. Yet only a miniscule breath to the taxi man. Did he really know so much about this girl's situation that he could anecdote each reply, predict each response. Hardly had Ele'hail's reaction been drawn than this egomaniac answered her back. Not a very good introduction to the art of conversation she thought. That was what I thought to reply she thought. Yet she had not uttered a word. And the man came out and said her thought! The subject was skimming between trust, denial, justification yet each thought process was pre-empted by a verbosity of such angst and fury that she could not get a word in edgeways.

The topic of co-laboration was dismissed. Each could listen not only his own words, but each other's thought responses. He was a kleptomaniac of all the thoughts she had ever encountered and he was not about to let her off the hook. What was the candour of the man's experience? She gathered that he was a kind of celestial taxi-cab driver and he mentioned a lot about angels. She had to read in between the lines. For this was conversation between dimensions where thoughts were pre-empted and conversation confused by the bending of the rules of physics. However, the light permeated and the man stopped what he was jabbering and attended to the portal. It went dark and he was gone- are all conversations with people that hard thought Ele'hail? For she had actually only spoken with her mother and father before. She wondered what had become. Her parents had been part of the universal substitution principle of *The Mnemic Eye* whereby they had been transformed into Ele'hail's wings. Their lives had become intertwined with hers and were contained within her beating wings.

It was the end of a life, to Michael and Velouria for this gosling minute could it be- the END? I wonder what the last musical sound will be. The ends of the earth. The apocryphal silence. The discord of elemental collapse perhaps, when rhythmic resonance, to the ear breaks the chord of intimacy the sound bears an incantation. True music of closeness. Or perhaps a slow peaceful exhalation of breath. A sigh. A crash, a cacophony of whispers. A deathly silence. There must be no sound in time. Time must have a stop. At the end of the world there will be only two sounds- harmony and discord. The harmony of a final pause. The discord of dread.

A celestial hum followed. Will gatherings of angels mark the final demise? Will there be a climax of life or a slow melody of decaying half-life, stuttering of the masses forming other masses persist. Will anyone be around to hear it? Will the swansong of life on earth be the unsung coming of the Lord in glory and phasing light? It was to them the acronym of a desolate bid for freedom amidst crescendos of Stravinsky and Shostakovich played amidst the clinking of glasses at the restaurant at the end of the universe.

They found themselves all at once surrounded by a host of dancing daffodils. They stood, feeling the breeze, the root tendrils making the ground shimmer between them and nature. The dark sods of earth beneath sustained its stillness. When soft daffodil, open to the virus breaks, the heir of intimacy sees as imitation the true art of closeness.

They could not move, not like the children, the children they watched from its still vantage place as it stretched, never realising but promising spring. The delicate lines of its petals broke the air like a bell resounding, like a sole survivor of a great flood; proud and in many ways unsubstantial in the daybreak. Its colours were leant by the sun, its smell by the fairies. It was a cup of its own liquor, almost drunk on its realisation of life.

Life was short, life was fulfilling. It had a span which dealt in moments, not months or days. It was a focal point to the children who passed it, who asked inquisitively of its youth or colour. It was a statue of its own beauty. A so enticing miracle of spring standing still. Thickly remembering hallelujah out on the parade ground: regimentation was charm in the world of the solitary daffodil to the host surrounding. Then came the angels, yonder breaking from the form of the daffodil.

The communication of intimacy as the soul alights revelation of the true grace of closeness with God. In life it was a small bubble of air neath a pillow of dreams. It was the open suitcase at the start of a holiday, the heady excitement of the pleasure of freedom. It was the stare of a girl, the meditative swirl, and the antics of a horse running because he wants to. The foothold in virtue. It was the look of a child sitting content. It was the content of a Chinese takeaway. The taking away of pain, the replenishment of life. The affirmation of a kiss, the consequences of a wish. It was everything and nothing, the spark of recognition, the suppliance of a thought. It was the breath of God. But what do I do with it? In life I will not fear. With it I will not find fault. With it I will not search for self. With it I will glorify my support. I will just let it be. In death I will not fear. With it I will not find fault. With it I will not search for self. With it I will glorify my support. I will just let it be.

*The very cherubs huddled all together, like birds when soars the falcon and they felt a tingling to the tip of every feather and formed a circle like Orion's Belt around these poor charges of many coloured flames, until its tinges reached the speck of earth and made new aurora borealis spread its fringes.* ©Byron The motion of time played in their wings and they shone like the glare from the sun in a mirror so that one could not comprehend their features but one could feel their love and compassion from their voices which valued and gave triumphant feelings to them. The cherubs expressed choices to them, testing but feeling their way into his and her inner calm and serenity. He felt them lift him up and show him what his life was worth and what he needed to do for his daughter in the world of men. He felt a rush of insight in his conduct and below him a lone man conducting the elements with a baton and the squirmish of battle raged with the low calls of his daughter for guidance and help. They had a destiny still, away from the angels and they took the mantle given with hope and renewed spirit. There was still a place for them in the world. They would take the form of guide his daughter on her journey contained within her lofty thoughts. They would be a conduit to let her know the values she had to keep to reach her accomplishments; to let liberty's bell ring out all over the world of Miserablenow. The taxi-man opened the portal and Michael and Velouria returned to Heaven.

## Chapt. 13 Illumination of Conviction

The illumination of the sea greeted Ele'hail that morning. She had fallen asleep by the waves and awoke to the tide lapping around the sadness at her feet. *How fast thou fliest, 0 Time, on Loves swift wings, to hopes of joy, that flatters our desire: which to a Lover still contentment brings; yet when we should enjoy, thou dost retire. Thou stay'st thy pace (false Time) from our desire when to our ill thou hast'st with Eagles wings: slow only to make us see thy retire was for Despaire, and harme, which sorrow brings. 0 slake thy pace, and milder passe to Love, be like the Bee, whose wings she doth but use to bring home profit; masters good to prove, laden, and weary, yet againe pursues. So, lade thy Selfe with hony of sweet joy, and do not me the Hive of Love destroy.* ©Lady Mary Wroth. There was a hush over the land of Miserablenow. It was as though the people had woken from a misguided sleep and were dazed in their routine, functioning but not recognising their potential. In the absence of Amaeigin the power vacuum was being filled by Misericordia, lover of Amaeigin and her ally, Xtopherus. To Ele'hail life was a stretch of beach, her recent past before her and the sea her present and the sky her future. As she stared at the grey line of sand, the grey line of sea and the grey line of sky, she was calmed and the spring sun warmed her wings.

Craggy visions, slow denial of her sense of belonging, Misericordia had stood apart and cast out from Christianity. It was like this in so many years that she made a pact. A pact with the creatures that run and denote the foul stench of promiscuity. She went down a rabbit hole and pulled the clenched, decapitated small rabbits from their nests and devoured them. However, the night grew in intensity and as she was sitting scraping the bloody residue from her hands, she noticed her legs turning to jack-hammer bunny legs. She grew a fluffy white tail from her back and her teeth turned whitish-greyish buck toothed. She was a spectre of the night, a fascinating corrupt rabbit-woman!

Her days of exile had made her able to infiltrate the dreamworld of the populace. She hid in dreams forever banished from those who cared and was able to confront, seedy and salubrious, the suitors of the world she left behind to follow her onto the plains where the warrens were. There she would fall upon their pithy souls picking the words from their very mouths and filling their sleeping corpses with the bile of their misdeeds. She would free their misconceptions and return them with their bodies fearful and lost in a world in which they no longer belonged. They would then hunt the world from which they were enslaved from and produce woe and misery. In this way the rabbit queen was able to corrupt the populace and re-enable her return. When she returned, she was welcomed as a dream. As a vision. She was the burning of nightmares. She was the dark side of the moon.

Ele'hail was not alone. There were the early soaring gulls strutting over the sand. They rose and fell with the wind and harassed each other in the barren sky. She rose to greet them and they wheeled and glided with her on the wind. She copied how they swept over the waves floating on the air currents and dipping her feet in the sea line. She felt like queen of the birds: *a spirit of a different aspect waved her wings, like thunder-clouds above some coast whose barren beach with frequent wrecks is paved; her brow was like the deep when tempest-tossed; fierce and unfathomable thoughts engraved eternity on her mortal face and where she gazed, a gloom pervaded space.*© Byron She had sampled their skyways and she soared with them sweeping eventually to the tower, unencumbered by isolation. Was her flight to encourage understanding, or revel in the realms of the airborne? *The natural function of the wing is to soar upwards and carry that which is heavy up to the place where dwells the race of gods. More than any other thing that pertains to the body it partakes of the nature of the divine.* ©Plato

Frustrating was it that Misericordia's plans were held in check by religion; plans that were thwarted by the convicted rebel Methuselah. He had been a great rebel leader and wanted to make amends for Amaeigin's treatment of both religion and the people. He sought to relieve the populace from Misericordia's dreamlike grip over them. He was imprisoned at the tower in Ingatestone while the plains from Ingatestone to Leytonstone were under Xtopherus's control. However sympathetic to Methuselah were the forest dwellers of Epping Forest who cut a swathe through her power base and thwarted Misericordia's ambition to rule the dreamland by their earth wisdom and passages of Christianity which Methuselah had reinstated in the forest.

Ele'hail turned to the illuminator (who had been known as Dionysius in his mortal life and had shown such corrupt but merciful ways as a leader of men that he had been assigned to this role in the afterlife) for company being too naïve to approach any living human. He seemed a jolly and rather upbeat character who hid his melancholy well and only exuded joys and seriousness. He had seen many an angel descending from heaven and it gave him the perspective of controlled wisdom with the humility of those who could answer riddles of time. Indeed, Ele'hail asked him many questions of why the world relied upon the angelic presence and why they bothered with us mere mortals.

"Angels are here" he said "to illuminate God's work and to encourage conviction, whether in the sense of vengeance or mercy. Angel means messenger of God and it is in His instructions that they are formed. They are extensions of God and so are you to enact God's and so ultimately our plans. Angels help heal our peace of mind through their light and and provide an ego-free measure by which to repel fear and approach situations through love. He then said a prayer, "For remember" he said, "you can petition them through prayer- *We have our treasure in earthen vessels, but thou O holy spirit, when thou livest in a man thou livest in what is infinitely lower. Thy spirit of holiness, thou livest in the midst of impurity and corruption* please bring the angels here to bring us faith; *thy spirit of wisdom, thou livest in the midst of folly,* please bring the angels here to educate us; *thy spirit of truth, thou livest in one who is himself deluded,* please bring the angels here to heal us. *Oh, continue to dwell there, thou who dost not seek a desirable dwelling place, for thou wouldst seek there in vain. Thou creator and redeemer make a dwelling for thyself; oh continue to dwell there that one day thou mightest finally be pleased by the dwelling which thou didst thyself prepare in my heart, foolish, deceiving and impure as it is.*© Kierkegaard You see we have a lot to go through before we are worthy of them but the more you want, or rely on them the more their influence grows; so that for some they illuminate a hairs breadth and that is enough, while others are given wings and they illuminate a whole lot more."

The illuminator tended to the portal and was gone. It was only his manner which Ele'hail thought upon and that of the angels' demeanour shone through him. She retired into her parents' bedroom which was exactly how they had left it. Ele'hail perched on the bed and opened a secret clasp from which sprang a drawer. It contained letters from Michael and the crispness of the paper tingled her hands. She read of Methuselah who had been a calm and Christian council to them both. He was a sympathetic figure and as such the letters illuminated the conviction that she should seek him out. She also found a map to Michael's forest lair and she decided it was time to visit both. She read out loud from one of the letters and felt their convicted sense of togetherness which had sustained her for so long:

> Forest Cavern
> Peddlers Wood
> Frinton
> Miserablenow

dec. ad603

Dearest Velouria

For now, I realize why Xtopherus spoke to you of the moon, its orbit the luminous path across the sky which exists only for the womb's stirring. Maybe I am just going crazy for a shroud of cloud is like the flower which lifts up a young girl's cloudlike arms as she prepares for bed. You dream away the cold moon like a snow laden tree with wicked gravity shelters the traveller. How should I formulate theory, on this new religious cult when the spectrum of feelings is compounded in your songs, like a romance in Christianity rests upon the passage, sung by the leading man as he wanders down his lover's street. Are there lilac trees in any other part of town?

Will there comes a time when I am driven from my empty bed and walk to your street as the snow falls and the amber night descends. I'd cuddle up to the moon and perhaps build you a snowman in the winter's porch and scratch and scream and prowl all night like the cats upon the street. Your joy would turn me into this creation for Angel rain is the ice-maiden, her flanks glistening in the snow, her icy wings the chill of night and her brown eyes the coming of dawn's early light. I would endure a thousand moons to be an entrance to your soul, your needful stare beckoning me in from the cold and yet in your sight I would gain entrance and linger, until I thawed, my body and love a fleeting gift with which I long to lay you down upon the white sheets of virgin snow. The girl who built me was smiling then and it was no coincidence.

I sit in my chair stroking the velvet as though it were St. Michael adjusting the gates of heaven. I can't get your eyes from of my head. I want to envelope my memory of you and become you, engulf the demons and show through pure and radiant, like a silver dragon on its way down your breast, a bead of sweat. I want the blame to be swept away on a lancing, thrusting note of pure reason. Of retribution for all those moments where you were not clear, not focused rather a scrunched-up piece of impudent feeling and hurt pride.

When you said an omnomatopia the first day I met you I knew you were no ordinary girl. I want to forgive and be forgiven, laugh and be laughed at, consume and be consumed, like a paper aeroplane floating over a sun-drenched garden, the speed, the intensity shouldn't matter just the beauty left behind. You know there are a few golden moments in life and when someone walks in strangers and leave as friends that is one. The hand that roams has been caught stealing ration books from the bureau. Its disposition was out of egotism or wantonness I don't know but he's in a right Greek tragedy caught lifting the covers off a long dead statue and no mistake. When we do your washing, I caress the fabric, which has been closest to your skin, as though I were having tea with Methuselah. My skin shivers at the thoughts the hand conjures, as I fear I will eventually seek out the more deliquesce regions of the female form; the waterfall you speak of is a crystal Italian stream, rushing translucent to engulf our kiss. Our degree of freedom. I beseech you not to inflame this young man's heart. For I adore you and would envelope words of love so poignant that time would be profligate next to a face such as yours, which can stop a clock. For science has overcome both space and time but you stop even the objection. A kiss from you would be heaven but never a heartfelt goodbye in this world of espionage and counter espionage. Oh! that we could go to the coastline and wait for Methuselah's boat hand in hand, shoulder to shoulder in this wild, dramatic and winking art.

Could I have swept you off your feet, talked to you of romance and dancing in winter playgrounds of the rich and famous and of the allure in your eyes? Instead, I walk like a pack horse at the lady of Shallot's side, while the gelding's parade and prance in your wake. Well, I've got the time if you've got the space between the cabined cells to be my fantastical Nazi-Italian spy lover whom I have to warn of impending danger as Velouria moves in to arrest her fellow spies. One of whom could be a rather quirky fellow called Xtopherus whom we have reason to believe was educated at the salon in Rome in the art of romantic entanglement and is as we speak under Velouria's private control. He kisses too well for a real homosexual! He will no doubt get others to join his sun-drenched liturgy to the saintly ghost of expensive Italian Christmas presents which drown the head of babies and douse a wound in vitriol, to heal the garish, apish stories of lovers leapt. (I heard a rumour that you tempt the sun to your windowsill and laugh as it attempts to sweep the remnants of succour into your room for, I have heard that you read to it naughtily worded poetry. What writhes beneath a stronger depraved passage like a codebook!)

Amaeigin only lines his own pockets with pearls where, searching for the sublime often appears spineless as well. Controversy doesn't really appeal to me and when thrown into the deep end my approach is to swim as near as I can to an athlete when we humans are a poor excuse for an animal, average at most things and prone to regret more than we excel. That's where you are different. You can be relative and absolute with a gesture or command. You really are far more honest than me and although you regret things now, they'll come a time when you'll be the queen of somewhere else you always knew you were. Queen of Miserablenow. Maybe the characters of somewhere else should get together and say improve. I guess I should appreciate what I am. I think therefore I am, so that the void is only a state of mind. Thanks for giving me a hug, I really appreciated that. I'll take it with me across the winds and spread a little love in Miserablenow. I used to be such a touchy-feely person when I was younger but who knows where the time goes, I have no need for time. I have only the need to give safe conduct through the world of your vulnerable soul growing;

Methuselah today said that I should deal with uncertainty and aim to seek conclusions to the criteria I have raised. Like how did I come to be here, within your love? Did Xtopherous give me the key to your secret pagan place? It would be just like him. I can thrive now that I have found my way home, now that I am free, now my arrow flies true, now I am with you and I feel the pride which comes from being given the lady's colours. As me, I will still fight for your honour and bleed for you until the heart of man is the pagan sacrifice. Heaven is just a word from the land of wine and plenty but words from your mouth sound like heaven so as long as I do not lead fallen angels to bed with you, I will live with the heaven of your words and I will unfold my jealousy with your words of honesty which hold me spellbound. But if I take you by the hand and tell you all I want to do is see you smile I hope you will understand. I said we were in a triangle but there are no straight lines between us and I guess as the ostrich taps at my window that I know what you've been thinking all along and your enthusiasm is like mine. But you can steam open the envelope of my soul and keep blood on the inside and nowhere else. For I do not need you to bleed for me. So, I will stand at your open window and imagine you in all your naked glory for me to touch and from the tree with seven leaves hold your embrace as a crowd holds the stone work of art. Your constancy is your song and if I listen, I can hear it in the tapping of the ostrich rain on my window. I swear if I listen to the rain I can hear your snog. I send you a baby kiss through the post and let the semi-circle of my lips be the paradise Isle you are dreaming of.

My tongue is silent, my pen still. Everything is well in Velouria's tower. Your thread resistance takes my feet off the ground as I unfurl your flag, which you have been busy spinning, like a dream. Lay it out of your window and I will know you have received this letter.

Love and Green

Michael

## Chapt. 14 Liberty's Quest

A boy walked around the edge of the lake, its rhododendron-redness seeping from the sun into the chill waters, sometimes with a purpose, at others with a languor so that the expanse of nature seemed but distant to his inner thoughts- *Wherefore, we know not, at times, far nearer things common come, and lineaments half-seen grow in a moment magically clearer;- perhaps, as he walked, the grass he called too green, rose rebuked him, or the earth ill-lighted silently smote him with the charms he slighted.*© A. Dobson Perhaps time like the light seemed dimmer then but he saw Ele'hail and with furrowed brow turned and looked into the lake. As she approached him, he pretended not to have noticed and sat swishing a stick at the weed. He looked curiously at her reflection behind him as she fanned her wings. He started and stared closer. Indeed, she had wings. She spoke "I have not seen a person this far east for ages she said- of where do you live?"

"I have come up the river with my father from the forests of Epping. Are you an angel?" she turned and unclear of purpose said

"I am but the girl I always was. My wings are," she paused; "natural to me. They are a blessing." They looked at a pair of mandarin ducks on the lake.

"I suppose your livery is practical" he said "not like the showy glare of the ducks."

"I think they are beautiful" she said "and yes if you mean can I fly, yes of course." The boy looked with wonder at Ele'hail but kept silent. There was a silence like a man admiring a great task he had finished and then suddenly the boy erupted:

"Well have you come from lands far away- have you come from the east beyond the sea, have you alighted on this spot just to talk to me- what is your purpose?"

"I am seeking a forest cave and also Methuselah. Have you heard of him?"

"Why of course- he is our leader in the dreamworld battles between the forest folk and Velouria. He displays courage but was lured into talks with her and was imprisoned in the tower at Ingatestone. Of the forest cave I have scouted this peddler's wood and found nothing."

"Come with me" Ele'hail said and disappearing into the wood's haze of bluebells looked up and down for a specific oak. Have you seen a great hollow oak surrounded by pollard beech trees?" She asked and he led her to a circle of trees ahead. As they walked, they were aware of their eyes misting into the bright blue of the flowers. "This is the gospel oak" she said and touched it as her father had many times. "It is a short distance." They came to an area of new growth and around a circle of saplings there was an entrance to an underground cavern. He brushed away leaves and opened a hatch. It creaked and they stepped inside.

It was as Michael had left it, with a small table in the centre and a bed, shelves etc around the walls. They sat down in the two chairs and after a moment began to realise that they were not really that different. Both had had the tree lore handed down to them from their fathers and they spoke of gateways and understanding from the oak, and the blackthorn a tree of hope and courage, and the alder the tree of balance, and the willow which Ele'hail had not seen, the tree of inspiration and intuition.

"Come down to the river and I will show you the willow" the boy said remembering that he would be missed by his father. "Later" she said. "I want to spend this night in the cavern- are you? -"

"I must go" said the boy, "my father will be searching for me. Bye!" and he left rather awkwardly. When he got to his father's boat he told him of the strange winged girl. His father looked at him understandingly and said;

"Yes of course". However, the boy was adamant and led his father back to the wood. In the dark however he could not find the cavern; for Michael had hidden it well.

So, what of Michael and Velouria? The temperance of heaven is such that time knows no common votary there. Indeed, they had become conductors of the elements. Hence it was as Ele'hail slumbered safe in the cavern that they were preparing for her momentous journey and seeding her dreams and the atmosphere with the ability and wish to fly to Ingatestone tower. Contained within her wings and her perceptions they worked their magic. When she awoke, she was sure that she would fly to the tower and secure Methuselah's release.

Leaving the earthy bonds is an opportunity to be cradled in the arms of nature, and lifting from the ground with a few powerful strokes she wound up over the forest, gained height, said goodbye to the gospel oak and glided over towards the fields and valleys of the river which led to Ingatestone and Epping Forest. Flying was to find the pressure gradient favourable and utilising muscle power to overcome density differences between the substance of body and the substance of air, lift overcame drag. Flight was controlled by her tertiary wing surfaces and in roll, pitch and yaw she had become experienced. She had reached these degrees of freedom and could soar subconsciously but all the while her wings were coping with these dynamics.

Her thoughts would be uplifted by her flight in that, even more than ground travelling, the process of her past was consolidated by the present effort and future destination. She was driven effortlessly forward by her speed and could sweep the future ahead of her when she dived or let sensation take over when she glided. She felt balanced and only just realised her conspicuousness as she rose over towns and villages.

The ground was becoming more populated as she flew onwards and she gained height until she could see Ingatestone tower in front of her. It was an imposing edifice in a lush valley and of the same proportions as Walton Tower. She circled around a couple of times and seeing only a solitary figure in the courtyard of the uppermost chamber she decided that this must be Methuselah. She swooped down and observed the astonishment he showed as she broke from cover. She introduced herself as Ele'hail and Methuselah knew immediately who she was. He was a tall man with rolling eyes which pierced the air and held one in a steadfast gaze. She obviously looked excitable and couldn't keep still.

M: Beware! I sense that expressionate passion in you. I like just being by its outskirts; the shadow of your sparking fizzing from an inner calmness is enough.

E: 1 have come from the sea, staring into answers it holds, where nothing but the sea understands. I guess really, it's the agony and ecstasy I have to relate to, the white horses of the waves, not respond to one's own answers that always come free. Just let everything settle, it's good to have a friend, someone whose life you can try on for size for a while and to just get perspective.

M: Better still if that person can hold conversation like she were a bird holding gravity in swooping flight in fond honesty. What was left was how you have been feeling recently. A kind of emergence to level ground, sprung from a prison, with a downward spiral of loneliness on one side and the upward spiral of flight on the other.

E: I don't know about you but I want to join these two and fly away across the plain on the sultry breeze over the twin bonnie waters, till dawn rises, near as the sea moon resplendent.

M: You must learn to be logical

E: Create a mathematical certainty, like a matrix?

M: A matrix is a funny thing. It's a way of putting equations together and determining the roots of them. Mathematically it solves unknown parameters. I think your matrix will define the unknown, though whether you choose to accept them is of course up to you. I regard the esteem I hold for you to be similar to the way a girl holds the mysteries of nature beyond the society which keeps her from being real, and the tension that keeps her from sleep.

Ele hail looked blank

-You have to try logical, lateral, tangential and spiralling in thoughts so as not to confine your creativity. Inspiration will come it's just that by definition it is an intangible and fragile and illusionary answer which relies too much on the latter. I found logic of the gospels, the lateral thoughts of the psalms, the tangential thoughts of the proverbs and the spiralling thoughts of revelations- a great inspiration to me.

E: The tortured soul is definitely the spice of life, humanism, genius- looking over the edge and quite enjoying the view. But you must manage it through the bible so your dreams will not desert you to galvanize you into moving on.

M: I read the news today, oh boy, 4000 holes in Miserablenow. Dreams eh. I think dreams are like holes- you explore the depths but don't realize you are in one. I often dream of naughty men. Big strong manly types who are basically riddled with guilt over the decisions they make. Amongst my friends there are special, compassionate and genuine people but my patience wears thin with so-called real men and people who try too hard. We should learn from Jesus and instil a little hometown friendliness.

E: But I love dreaming, I want to hide myself away

M: That's why you sleep so much- because the world = outside world is so cruel and reality is overrated. In sleep everything combines and you appear to have a much-homed conveyance of creativity in behaviour potential than in another world in which you want to fight the fears aroused by danger. Dreaming is a great way of doing that though.

E: I am alone now; my parents have transfigured into my wings by the magic of the Mnemic spiral trees. I have given up on them and am in a mind maze.

M: You said you gave up your parents but feel pure. You really need to embrace your moral viewpoint because what they constructively sacrificed is for the best in the end. Hopefully you will be completely free from its wrath if you play your hand and think sequentially what is best. You're doing it now. We live in one world in one day so don't try to recover everything all at once; it probably won't be perfection yet.

E: And how will I lead, take over the seal; to chase perfection until it becomes your world for you can't be all things to all people. Belief in your mind will open the door but the door is a portal to what you think is right for you.

M: You said we were in a maze and you're right and it's something we can construct and has always been. Just for one moment I thought I'd found my way but as destiny unfolds, I saw it slipping away. But not now. It's no maze you are a sign that we can take back MISERABLENOW! There's something in your eyes, which is so hopeful that I believe in you. No words could explain, no action could determine just being you. We were both imprisoned against our will. Yet you can fly. Oh wonder. Could you fly me away from captivity?

E: Flying. That comes naturally for me. Climb on my back and we will escape!

Circling over the grassland between the town and forest Ele'hail waited for Methuselah's procession. As it entered the forest, she tracked it by swooping low over the tree canopy. Methuselah was greeted by a throng of people appearing then disappearing into the forest so that by stealth and camouflage they had never been there. The entourage grew and Methuselah beckoned to Ele'hail to land in Loughton camp which loomed from the canopy. It stood on a promontory amidst a swathe of ancient trees and surveyed the surrounding area. By foot one came upon it quite stealthily but from Ele'hail's vantage point it seemed to command the area like a general in battle. As they approached bells began to peel out: *A single church below the hill is pealing, folded in the mist: ring out old shapes of foul disease; ring out the narrowing lust of gold; ring out the thousand years of old, ring in the thousand years of peace. Ring in the valiant* Ele'hail *and free, the large heart, the kindlier hand; ring out the darkness of the land, ring in the Christ that is to be.* ©Tennyson.

As Ele'hail landed by a brook which ran through it she was surrounded by the people who took refuge there. The boy whom she had met in Peddlers Wood sprang up and heralded her with a call to arms. "To all gathered here this is Ele'hail!" he said, "the heir of Miserablenow." She showed them the seal ring and there was a hush. Soon Methuselah ushered her to a tent by his large imposing hall and spoke to the assembled crowd of how she had survived the great fire in Walton and how she had rescued him from the clutches of Misericordia at Ingatestone Tower. A few were allowed discourse with her to give seal to disputes or plan the heralding of the arrival but the enclosure for her provided the rest she needed from the harrowing flight.

In the evening, they sat around an impressive fire and Methuselah told her of the plans for her to become the figurehead between the populace of the towns and plains ruled by Xtopherus and the forest dwellers led by himself. Xtopherus was alienated by Velouria and needed trade to resume between his towns and the forest highways which were blocked from his passage. When word was sent then of the arrival of Ele'hail it was just the chance he had been waiting for to sign a treaty and end hostilities. He was a troubled man with an independent will but had been subdued by the influence in dream and council of Misericordia, the rabbit-woman. They met later that week:

E: I have come from Walton tower in the valley of mist and have touched the bright coloured lights of the angels who adorn us with a gentle passion to fill our eyes with hope that I can only smile upon

X: The moon is sad this night a sullen glow tells heavily upon our hearts but we see nothing but true happiness in your telling soul, for you return the seal to the kingdom
The field is torn by her wish. My dreams fall to the warrens due to Velouria's grip.

E: Yours will rise from that lowly place for what is higher than time through sun moon noon. Dreams are heavier with the influence of Misericordia but we will succeed until the very end when our hearts are tired of this life. Stars will shine for us then and mine will shoot, always to be in the light.

*X: The pulse of void central, yes, I can still hear it. The echoes are playing tricks on my ears; me, the black and the shaft of light. Here I am entering the light, so strong that no shadows emerge.*

E: It is the light of love, transcending all.

*X: Love is weakness of character. Love is selfish. Love is dangerous. Love is unrequited. Love is the ultimate sacrifice yet- loveless life is the greatest cynic. I justify to myself that the morals and ideals that I have been fed by Velouria are not always the ideals of the others around you. Many people have different perspectives; many are not compatible. All the void, it seemed so far away and Velouria's song was so powerful* (when Ele'hail sighed) *and life seemed null. I feel it is Velouria; is some form of torture, in her crystallised form. She is the apparition with me in her arms. The butterflies they emerge from my coffin! Humanity in its insignificant vessel reaches out into the void.* © Oliver Dachinger

Ele'hail knew that she would have to rid the kingdom of Misericordia and she set about preparing for when their dreams would collide. Methuselah and Xtopherus finished the treaty and each went back to their stronghold content and with a song which transferred hegemony to Ele'hail: "Thou art the star to light my way, turning my path from night to day. Thou art my joy, my grief, my sorrow, my hope of grace today tomorrow. Thine is the power and can relieve all fears and bring me lasting peace. Peace comes from there and joy wending quiet repose all else transcending. Crowned by thy love, life has meaning, thy shining glance thy soul revealing, with courage high I raise again triumphant in a world of pain. Thou art the star to light my way turning path from night to day."

## Chapt. 15 Ele'hail is Victorious

As Ele'hail approached the dark tower of Ingatestone she felt the rabbit tracks furrow her brow. Misericordia was asleep in the tower. The rabbit-woman that knew its own sin, lived by that rule. It could not delude itself into thinking it acted out of anything but wanton lust. Lust, which was the temptress of desire, the concrete of deceit, the unrighteousness of the rabbit. It likened to go out and kill, its face an ugly mask rapping at your sleep- need you live when you can dream? Ele'hail was uplifted but its heights knew only depravity and rage. It was as a demon seed blowing upon the wind ever attracted to that which was pure and delineated by pulling its victims into the concrete their desires formed.

Ele'hail was the creative glimpse of purpose. She shows the point of trying. The point of sharing. The need of knowing. See your sky feathered into masked glory billowing from the moon drops of ivory as she flapped her wings in the brightness of the chamber to startle Misericordia but Misericordia soon recovered to use her guile and conceit to enter bonds and infiltrate desire. Feel the moonglow sob. She would wait until she gave of her very soul before she would strike and drag her talons, flesh wise into her forgiving breast; wriggle rabbit like inside her nightgown. People thronged with rasping breath to see her bloodlust. In concrete then all was lost for the union would be encased in wrath and finish with short eager contamination of the bed which sealed fate.

Such Ele'hail moved in a butterfly's gasp; the wings that roamed full of the giggling naive compassion of a vision sealed in innocence. She swooped down to her bed chamber. Misericordia's dreams caressed the firm ripe joints of the victim, cajoled and harried the prey until it was trusting and its loyalty faded into a patch full of secrets. She told of the world of men to be welcomed but not, understood. She pulled her wings towards the concrete to encase them for posterity- dampened state, soon to hear them crack- another dream victim! Yet then Ele'hail rose and from up high swooped as the kestrel and pinned the rabbit-woman to the floor. She moved in for the kill. Dreams spiralled faster faster, hear them pant, slower slower, death imminent.

Michael and Velouria were on the hillside commanding the elements and conducting the dreams of the rabbits. "Do not make me love in vain" and with that Misericordia flinched, rolled over and stopped breathing. For even she had come to love Ele'hail. Her heart could not cope. Its foreign body to her ways was her death Knoll and pain was wrestled away from her concrete grip.

Previously the pain was just a dream. Today pain was washed away by the rain. Would there be an impact of responsibility to do what we chose and what if that was evil? If we practise choice, it has an effect on others and our relationships. Amaeigin had a choice, from within which were abominable notions that the wren would recognise then flew to where they know not. Plucked from marrow in the land of Miserablenow; Velouria had placed in others' lives goodness, and in honour and respect Michael followed her. In virtue Ele'hail's wings of feathers, plumes of hair born in glory rose from the relationship. The murmured cloud, the silence of fear diminished and the respite of confluence with the soul turned to sensitive appraisal of Ele'hail's virtue. Did the ball therefore stop in the air for a moment? Did the baton conduct perfection? The gravity of the exposition ceased turmoil in the mind. Peace descended over Miserablenow. Ele'hail crowned the Queen of Miserablenow. Over those from the sea, the plains and the forest. Even over those from the rabbit warrens of despair. In that way innocence overcame madness and Ele'hail completed the song in the key of concrete.

www.ingramcontent.com/pod-product-compliance
Lightning Source LLC
Chambersburg PA
CBHW030343030726
47499CB00003B/882